THEN THE DARK

MARKUS MURPHY BOOK 2

MIKE MCCRARY

MIKE McCRARY

THEN THE DARK

For them.

"Rule your mind, or it will rule you." – Horace

"I punched my mother out once." – Charles Manson

THE NIGHT EVERYTHING CHANGED

CHAPTER 1

Nice, quiet Cody Higgins whispers a gentle prayer as he loads the dishwasher.

Prays the gun doesn't slip out from his pants.

He's comfortable and uncomfortable with the weapon.

Cody was given the gun yesterday. Or maybe she gave it to him a few days ago—he forgets exactly when Lady Brubaker handed it to him. Things have gotten beyond fuzzy lately, but he'll never forget the feeling that rippled under his skin as she handed it to him.

A jolt of electricity.

He was frightened, excited, and so, so proud.

Hasn't fired it yet, but he has a strange confidence in his skills. There's this chunk of unearned knowledge he holds. A crystal-clear vision of how to work the weapon at a very high level is present inside his mind. Yet, at the same time, there's no clear memory of ever pulling the trigger on anything in his life. As if he knows he's a master marksman while never having taken a shot before.

She chose him.

That's what's important.

Lady Brubaker wouldn't handpick nice, quiet Cody Higgins if he couldn't do it.

"So, you'll be gone how long?" Jennifer Higgins, Cody's wife, glances over. A mix of puzzled and annoyed.

"An hour? Perhaps slightly more. Two at a maximum." Cody shuts the dishwasher, adjusting the gun with his back still turned to her. "Have to go into the office for this." He smiles. "It's a silly, boring project. You wouldn't be interested."

"Oh, that's not true." Jennifer flashes some fake curiosity while not bothering to look up from her phone. Her fingers feverishly tap away at a conversation with someone else. "If it's important to you..."

Cody nods.

He lets the quiet fill the room, expanding like a balloon.

Cody won't be quiet or nice for very much longer.

Taking in a deep breath, he opens the door. Doesn't trouble her with saying goodbye. His thoughts turn to what will happen while he's gone. He knows what plan Jennifer has already set in motion. Knows with absolute certainty who her fingers are having that conversation with while he washed the nightly dishes. This has been going on for some time. He shuts the door behind him and exhales.

Hope she has fun.

There's a chill in the air as he steps out into the driveway. Feels nice. Lights are on in the windows of the homes that line the Higgins's street. Well-manicured yards. The occasional bark of a dog mixed with sounds of children playing the next street over.

He closes his eyes, feeling the cool breeze push across his face. Helps him shift the mental gears in his head. Lets things slip, slide, then grind into their proper place. Moving away from Cody Higgins. A chump of a husband. Neighborhood nobody and almost-senior project manager at Blah Blah Corp working on blah, blah, whatever automated pricing controls system. There's a shift in his jumbled head. A click. Thoughts begin to race toward what he has been chosen to become.

His fingers touch the gun under his shirt.

He squeezes the handle through the fabric.

Didn't realize he was even touching the weapon until the hair on the back of his neck stands up straight and tall. His heart pumps harder and harder. Closing his eyes, he envisions the plan. Knows it by heart. He'll take the train into the city, walk a few blocks, hop on a bus, then get off at Central Park.

There's a protest in progress.

An unrest rising across the city. Across the nation. Yes, Lady Brubaker chose nice, quiet Cody Higgins to fire off a revolution.

He opens his eyes, turning to see his dear wife through the window.

She's all smiles now that Cody has left the house. Tapping away on her phone.

Cody will be back to kill her soon.

CHAPTER 2

CODY HIGGINS REVIEWS the plan one last time as he adjusts his wig.

The bush of ratty hair plays a little on the homeless side of things but that's sort of the idea. His own hair is nothing to crow about. His normal look leans more toward undecided hippie than cool hipster. He slips on a pair of round glasses—not his —that are part of the illusion. The ratty-haired wig, the glasses, and the dirty T-shirt he pulled on after he hopped off the train are all part of his silly disguise. Much needed, but silly nonetheless.

He and several others met with Brubaker moments ago.

A final walk-through.

A dry run.

It wasn't a long meeting, but it was enough.

Just to be near her. To be in the same space sharing the same air. Those eyes. Those wonderful tattoos that run along those sculpted arms of hers. It was almost too much for Cody to take. To hear her words coming from her lips. Her strength. Her intelligence. Following her to the gates of hell is a trip Cody would gladly take.

Cody's role in the plan is simple.

Not easy, but it is simple. He will do what needs to be done at the park, then wait. Just wait, because no matter what happens—good or bad— Cody is to go to a safe house exactly one week from tonight. If there is a change, he will be contacted via the encrypted phone she gave him. He knew better than to ask questions. There was no need.

Brubaker has been right about everything so far.

Central Park is up ahead. It buzzes like a hive. People scream protests. Calls for change. The pulsing energy of rage fills the night air.

Cody's fingers tingle as he cuts through the crowd.

His body vibrates with excitement. There's this neglected part of him that aches. One that simply can't wait to unleash. Burning to go on a rampage. As if this other half of him has been holding back. The mix of drugs Brubaker gave him at the meeting has evened him out to some degree, but there's been a blend inside his mind. The balance is tricky. Actually, the balance has slipped and tipped toward the dark since the meeting. Who he was and who he's become has no line dividing them any longer. That vanished in the blink of an eye.

Cody touches the gun again as he pushes through the masses gathered at the park. He's been warned about the feelings he will have.

Warned about the moment that he will see *him*.

Told it will be beyond strange. How could it not be? How does someone reconcile seeing the person who has been added to you? The person who's been mixed into your mind against your will. The madness of a trained killer that's been jammed into your nice, quiet existence. They flooded Cody's mild mind with a psychopath's wild thoughts. His experiences. His skills.

Yes, Cody imagines it will be quite strange to see Markus Murphy alive and in the flesh.

They won't have time to chat, he knows that, but it would be nice to talk to him.

In the distance up ahead, he can see people being pushed aside as Brubaker cuts through the crowd. Warmth spreads through Cody's chest at the sight of her. Two men follow her while on their phones. One man turns, looking back and to the right. There's a cop on his phone standing in the middle of a footbridge. The cop is only about ten feet from Murphy, who's with a woman.

The sight of Murphy stops Cody dead in his tracks. Cody is in position. This is where he's supposed to be, but he is frozen. Stuck in place, unable to move. His arms feel like concrete. His breathing is labored. *Beyond strange* doesn't cover it. Like seeing part of yourself in a different body. Watching a version of yourself standing in Central Park, unaware you're even there.

Murphy is scanning the area.

The cop on the bridge is looking right at Murphy. The cop's focus is singular. A cold, dead stare on Murphy as the cop pockets his phone. Cody knows the cop, knows he is no officer of the law. This cop was at the meeting with Lady Brubaker. *Set it off* is what she told them all.

Cody almost feels bad for what is about to happen.

Sorry for those in the park who are not with them.

The cop on the bridge breaks into a chilling smile while staring at Murphy. The cop must feel it too. Feel his part in this. His part in history. The cop's back goes straight. His eyes shift to crazed as he drags a finger across his throat.

Cody pulls his gun. Takes a deep breath.

The cop pulls his gun, shooting a man unfortunate enough to be closest to him.

The crowd screams.

Cody raises his gun. Squeezes the trigger.

His perfect shot removes the cop's head. Sends him tumbling down, landing on the sidewalk a few feet from Murphy. People scream. Murphy whips around, pulling his Glock.

Cody can't believe it.

He made a perfect headshot from a considerable distance. Not a shot an amateur could make with a handgun. Not one an amateur could successfully pull off during the heat of the moment. Only a handful of people on the planet could make that shot.

Murphy could make that shot.

Cody made that shot.

There's a strange moment of calm. The park goes eerily quiet. Not for long, only lasting for a blink. But it was there. A tiny pulse of peace under the stars. Perhaps the last moment of calm they will ever know.

The volume jumps. Intensity grips tighter. The energy of violence has arrived. Police sirens wail.

Lights flash like electric red and blue gumdrops popping in the night. Officers draw their weapons, screaming for peace. Ordering calm. The crowd scatters in all directions with the roar of madness rolling across the park.

More gunshots ring out.

Bullets zip from all directions. Hard to tell where they are all coming from, or from whom. Another officer goes down, as does another civilian. A woman's leg blows out from under her. A pinata of flesh and bone. A large man takes a shot to the shoulder, spinning like a top to the ground. A cop chokeholds a man in a suit. No way to understand who's doing what in the swarm of men and women. Good and bad hard to parse. A tangle of bodies moving, jumping, charging, falling in every direction.

Cody runs hard, cutting through the crowd, leaving the park as fast as he can.

There's a car waiting for him with keys secured under the passenger side door.

All part of the plan.

Set it off, indeed.

Cody can hear Jennifer's moans and groans through the door.

The huffs and puffs of Edward.

Edward from down the street.

Nice, quiet Cody has known for months. Jennifer and Edward aren't as smooth as they think they are. A broken smile creeps across his lips as he grips his gun. He thinks of the shot he made at the park. Feels the chaos it caused. He allows that feeling to fill his heart all over again. Thinks of Murphy. Thinks of what he has become. A new man, as they say.

Cody is no more.

His life will be forever changed, and that change starts with correcting the situation behind this door. They must have closed the door, thinking that in some pathetic way they are keeping things private. They must think he's so stupid. Oh, how they must giggle about poor, weak Cody as their tongues and fingers play. He waits for Edward to finish. Not sure why. The animalistic noises fade into spent laughter.

He presses his tongue to the roof of his mouth, then kicks in the door.

Jennifer and Edward sit straight up in bed. Edward holds out his hands as if begging for time. Babbling about how Cody should be cool about this. Jennifer is shocked at first, then she laughs. Edward tries to silence her, but she keeps laughing.

Cody starts to laugh too. Laughs until his face turns red and he begins to choke.

Then he shoots Edward.

The back of Edward's head explodes in a bloody plume across the headboard. The boom of the gun is jarring. His ears ring. Much different than the openness of the park. An unmistakably uncommon sound in this perfect, storybook neighborhood. Jennifer's jaw falls open, broken words escaping from her mouth. Her entire body trembles. Cody lowers his gun. His eyes dark and blank.

"Cody—"

"No." He shakes his head as the remains of a laugh escape him. "No. Cody Higgins doesn't work here anymore."

"Please—"

"When the police reach our home..." He considers, smiles, then, "Jennifer, listen to me, please. Please tell them Mr. Madness was here."

"What?"

Mr. Madness shoots Cody's wife in her bare thigh.

CHAPTER 3

A SHOTGUN BLAST rattles the windows of the house.

A hollow echo rolls through the amazing home that's nestled in Montauk, New York.

The Mega Three came here to talk. The wealthiest, most powerful tech gods and goddesses the world has ever known have come here to find a solution to all that's gone wrong. Brubaker came here with a death squad to torture and gain information from them while the insanity at Central Park escalates.

Two members of that death squad stand in silence upstairs.

Tinker and Hiro wait, listening, still as statues.

There's a fight downstairs. An armed conflict

between their friends and him. That *him* has turned the rest of their squad into a bloody mess. Markus Murphy is downstairs. There was always an outside chance Murphy might be killed in Central Park. But they all know, deep down, there was no real chance of that happening. They know this because they are part Murphy too. And Murphy is the only one who would come here and be able to do what they're hearing downstairs.

There's been yelling.

Gunfire.

Dull thumps of bodies dropping.

Tinker's usual manic pace is forced into a motionless state. His wiry frame vibrates. Like a lid on a pot of boiling water. Hiro stands tall in the corner. A grizzly bear of a man in the middle of a slow burn. His breathing is steady and even. Silence is Hiro's steady state, but even the quiet giant wants war. His knuckles softly pop as he squeezes his fists tighter and tighter.

The stares between them communicate the best they can.

They want to join the fight. They want rage.

They steal glances between one another. Their eyes bounce to the guns and cash on the bed. They've watched the rest of their team go downstairs one by one. Even the weak one. The one who didn't turn out so good from the lab. Tinker begged him to stay. Tinker tried to protect the weak one, knowing Murphy would lay waste to him as if swatting a fly. Tinker and Hiro counted the shots fired and the sounds of the dead falling.

Tinker and Hiro are all that remain of this once proud squad of death.

Brubaker took them both aside in the meeting before Central Park, told them to survive above all else. Run if things got too spicy. Her word—*spicy*. She talked about him. About Markus Murphy. The man who is part of Tinker and Hiro, as well as the dead bodies piling up downstairs.

Tinker remembers being a lawyer.

Hiro remembers working security for a Japanese CEO.

Those are now distant thoughts that fade farther and farther back, slipping into the void. Brubaker gave them pills to *even things out,* she said. They watched her talk to someone else. Carl or Cliff or something that started with a C. He looked like an undecided hippie. A nice, quiet, corporate drone who didn't know what he wanted to be.

Brubaker talked about Tinker and Hiro running if things got beyond control.

Control has certainly slipped beyond their

grasp, but neither of them wants to leave. Running is not in their chemistry. He—Murphy—wouldn't run. Never. They wave their guns wildly, doing their best to express their anger while remaining quiet.

Hiro breaks, rushes the door. Tinker holds up a hand as a stop sign. They have orders. Gently, he places his hands on Hiro's broad shoulders, looking up to meet his eyes. Tinker whisper-mouths the words, *Not yet.*

Hiro's teeth grind.

Tinker squeezes Hiro's shoulders tighter, lowers his chin and nudges his head toward the window.

We have to go.

Hiro burns. Thinks. Finally nods with his eyes squeezed tight. Tinker exhales. They will have another chance at Murphy. There's more work to be done. Fun to be had. Brubaker told them to meet at a safe house if things did indeed go the wrong way. To meet there in exactly one week. Tinker hands Hiro a stack of cash as he pockets what he can. Both grab guns and ammo from the bed. Money, guns, and bullets. Strong seeds for a new beginning.

They hear Murphy talking on a phone.

Sirens wail in the distance.
Tinker opens the window.
Spicy, indeed.

6 DAYS LATER

CHAPTER 4

Markus Murphy and Mother sit quietly eating pie.

Eyes are down, focused on the plates in front of them, but they are together, seated across from one another at a table in a tiny diner just off the highway. Forks click and scrape. Sad songs from days past play from unseen speakers sharing the same air as the competing scents of popping grease and browning crusts. This is a black-and-white checkered tablecloth type joint with a surly, burly waitstaff that offers small-town charm by way of a politely extended middle finger.

Perfect.

"Which shithole is this?" Mother shovels in a forkful of apple pie.

"Number nine." Murphy matches hers and raises her another forkful. "Pretty sure it's nine."

Over the last few days, they've been traveling the area in search of the perfect piece of pie. All from a list Mother picked up while she was in prison. A woman in the next cell over was an expert—at least that's what she said—and she talked all the time about touring the country once she satisfied her debt to the criminal justice system. A life spent eating pies from this *best of* list she'd carefully constructed.

Mother thought that sounded like a pretty good idea.

Never told the woman, but she did think it was a damn strong plan. It captured a lot of what a person with lost freedom dreams of—good food and untethered roaming. The woman with the pie list caught a makeshift blade between the ribs while standing in the lunch line one day. Had nothing to do with Mother, for the record. The woman bled out, but not before Mother got her hands on the list. Fast minds and quick hands that aren't slowed down by sentimentality do well inside prison walls.

Murphy and Mother discussed it for about two minutes when he picked her up. They decided this wandering plan of pies was better than anything else they could think of. They were both free for the first time in a long time. Perhaps free for the first time ever. Devouring the best pies America has to offer sounded pretty damn nice. Not to mention, it was a lovely way to honor Mother's fallen prison buddy.

This pie decision—as it would be known—also represented the first true agreement between the two of them. A nice crack in the ice that had chilled their relationship ever since sperm collided with egg.

It's only been a few days, and they may not have completely bridged the gap between them, but they have found some mighty good pie. Some flat-out amazing slices, actually. There have also been some so-so ones, and sadly some that were complete shit.

Murphy and Mother have no real plans. That's part of the plan. Eat pie, drive, and figure things the hell out. There's a lot that's happened. Taking time to decompress is not something either one of them has ever really done. Never spent any of that *quality time* together they've heard so much about other families doing.

"So." Mother sips some coffee. "Let me get this straight."

"Shoot." Murphy stirs his.

"You're Markus Murphy. But in a way, you're not. That right?"

"Murphy."

"What?"

"Murphy. Everyone calls me Murphy."

"I'm a Murphy too, dumbass."

"One, that was like three husbands ago. Two, if you're going to force me to call you Mother all the damn time, then you can call me Murphy." Forks another heap of pie. "Sound solid?"

Mother considers this, then nods.

The second agreement between the two of them. An avalanche of family growth.

"Yes, to answer your question. I'm Murphy but with someone else added to the mix. Blended into my brain, if you will."

"And this new boy that's joined the party is... *Noah?*"

"That's right."

"And Noah is a good person?"

"Real Mr. Nice Guy."

"A nice guy? In your skull? That must hurt like hell."

"He was a nice guy. From what I can gather. I guess now it's *we*... I don't know. Stop with the questions already. Killing me."

"He had a family?"

"Still does." Avoids her eyes. Looks back down at his plate.

Mother leans back, studying her son. There is something different about her boy but it's hard for her to really put her finger on it. He's always been a bit of a puzzle—a mean and nasty one—but this is much, much different. It's in his eyes. Always in someone's eyes, she knows. There's something that shimmers like kindness in there. Not something she's ever seen in her son before. Maybe not since he was tiny and still sweet.

She turns, trying to get different viewing angles of him.

"Stop." Crust crumbles from his lips. "You're not going to see him."

"You understand how batshit crazy this all sounds?"

"I do."

"You two are in the same head. The CIA jammed you two together in a lab. Like a goddamn cerebral PB and J."

"Slightly more complicated than that, but yeah, that's the stripped-down version."

"And all the whacko shit that's happened. The riots? Central Park? The Cash Clash, I think they called it—the money stuff? That was because of this Mr. Nice Guy's wife?"

"Just think of us as Murphy. It's easier for everybody."

"Fine. Everything almost burned to the ground, went straight to hell because of you two's wife?"

Murphy's eyes drift ever so slightly.

Mother scrunches her nose. There he is. Never seen hurt in her son's eyes before either. Usually only a dark, empty space where feelings should reside. Now she can see the difference.

"Sorry." She leans in. "You. The other *you* that's inside that dicked-up brain of my boy. You're the reason we're even having this conversation. You're probably the only reason my boy is even speaking to me right now."

"Here we go." Lets his fork drop with a clank.

"Thank you—whoever you are—thank you for making my son a moderately less shitty human."

"Can we not?"

"Thank you for having a sense of humor too. My boy wasn't funny. He thought he was. He wasn't. Not at all. But you, you're all right, Mr. Nice Guy. You, I like."

Murphy starts to say something. A voice from the back of his head tells him to stand down. That smiling, damn voice tells him to let her have her moment. She just got out of prison. This is confusing for her. Still confusing for us too. A slight tug on the tail of his brain lets him know he should pull back. Mr. Nice Guy Noah is always present, shepherding Murphy on how being a functioning human works.

Murphy gives a half smile, drinks some coffee, then touches his gun under his shirt. He won't shoot her. However, the thought of it does provide him some comfort.

Fingers off the gun, Mr. Nice Guy whispers from the corner of his mind.

Kidding. I'm only kidding, Murphy reassures him. *Sort of.*

His fingertips slip away from the gun. He smiles to his Mother. Eats some pie.

Mother eyes him up and down. "You know this ain't over," she says.

"What's that?"

"This thing. This thing with your head. Them out there."

"Them?"

"Feds. CIA. All that shit you were telling me about."

"It's over for me."

"Doubtful as hell."

"It's over." His words come out much harder and louder than he wanted. Didn't even notice his nails are digging into the plastic checkered tablecloth.

Mother stops off the boom in his voice. The sudden spark of wild in his eyes.

"I'm still dealing with some anxiety." Murphy peels his fingers from the plastic. Takes another bite of pie. "Still a work in progress."

"What's that now?"

"Anxiety. I'm feeling it. All of it."

"What kind of bullshit, pussy-chatter is that?"

"I was just talking to you about it. Not more than five minutes ago. Ya know, my condition is ripe with big-ass, fluffy bursts of anxiety."

Mother stares back blank as a sheet.

He realizes opening up to this woman is pointless. Murphy almost breaks his eyes trying to stop them from rolling.

"You said something about you having kids." She changes the subject so fast it hurts.

"Not now."

"I'm a grandmother?" Her smile beams.

"You're not."

"I kind of am."

"Kinda not at all. They are Mr. Nice Guy's girls."

"And he is you, so therefore, they are grandbabies of mine." Spark in her eyes. "Girls?"

He's never seen his mother this way. Ever. Is this actual glee? Has prison softened her up? He can't ever really recall her smiling, let alone the level of joy she's showing right now. Joy set off by the idea of her *sort of* grandchildren.

Murphy's mind hits pause. Thoughts of the girls drive a sharp spear point into his bouncing brain. Like stabbing a fish from a stream. He's avoided the thought of them while convincing himself that he wasn't avoiding thinking about them. Denial wrapped in barbed wire.

"I can't," he says, spreading his fingers wide on the table. Looking for calm in the storm. "I can't do this."

"Do what? Not be an asshole?"

Murphy squeezes his eyes tight. Counts to ten, finds a happy place. This is the simple, silly thing Dr. Peyton showed him. A calming exercise. Breathing in deep through his nose, then exhaling slow through his lips. Feels like there're cold fingers gripping tight around his heart.

Mother watches on. Unsure which way to go with this.

Murphy's mind fumbles for stable ground.

He counts. He releases his breath slow and easy. His eyes pop open wide and wild. Murphy and Mother stare at one another. Neither having any idea of what to do or say. Murphy blinks. His hands shake. He shakes them back, then forces a smile onto his face in an attempt to shift the vibe of the table back to stable.

Mother gives an unsure nod.

"Saw a couple of places when we drove in." Murphy tosses some bills on the table. "Let's go shed a few pounds of this bullshit, pussy-chatter anxiety."

CHAPTER 5

Waves break.

Crashing, clapping, then smoothing out into a gentle rhythm playing in the distance.

These soothing ocean sounds are pumped into the room from undetectable sources. The conscious mind knows they are synthetic, but they feel as real as anything. The walls of the room are a sophisticated, flawless LED display system designed to surround the subject in a calm, comforting environment. Ocean waves roll in and out, spreading all along the four walls at a hypnotic pace.

An engulfing peace.

The air is cool and crisp but never cold. A slight breeze that randomly activates based on an algorithm that collected air movement from three different beaches located in Malibu and Santa

Monica. The floor is a polished nondescript concrete. The room is lit so the walls of rolling water are the focus, but not so much that you'd focus only on them. Studies show people tend to look down toward their feet during taxing conversations. The typical person avoids eye contact during such tense chats. Those same studies suggest simply removing the view of one's feet below can help open up the subject's willingness to share.

There's a table made from cherry wood in the middle of the room. Its bumps, lumps and small imperfections are left on the surface. Nothing smoothed over. Imperfections on display allow the subject to relax any thoughts of what perfect might be. A table specifically chosen to sit in this room among the wave walls. A solid slab of wood in the middle of the ocean. This is a room crafted to make the uncomfortable comfortable. Keep heartbeats stable. Voices below screaming. Emotions opened but kept unelevated. An optimal environment for difficult discussions. The desired effect is an ocean-side conversation with someone who wants to help.

Dr. Peyton enters the room.

She takes a seat on a steel stool with a plush, black leather cushion. She brought no pen. No pad of paper. No electronic tablet. Everything in the room will be recorded, of course—audio, video, the vitals of the participants—but the illusion of one-on-one communication is beyond important here.

It's everything, actually.

Peyton sits. Clears her throat as she places her palms flat on the table. She counts to ten, finds a comforting thought, much like she suggested to Murphy. She silently reaches ten. Her pulse is still up. Her shoulders are hovering around her ears like earrings.

It's not working at all.

Releasing a deep sigh, she looks to the wall, bites her lip, then nods.

Agent Irving strolls in with a casual strut. On the back end of his thirties, the tall gentleman with slicked-back hair moves like this is a bar. There's a noticeable scar on his otherwise perfect olive skin. A two-inch-long slice from a fight survived. Peyton heard he almost lost the eye during an operation that went bad not long ago. Kept his eye, but an agent he was close to was killed that day. Brutally, she heard. Peyton wanted to ask him about it but decided not to push.

"She's out there. Good to go." Irving's eyebrows bounce. "She's a goddam delight."

"Thank you." Peyton nods. "Appreciate the color."

He lowers his chin while pressing his lips together. An *are you sure about this?* gesture.

Peyton takes a moment. She forces her shoulders down, gives an unsure smile, then nods again. Agent Irving shrugs. He tried. He raises his hand, twirling a finger in the air.

A beat that seems to last forever.

A door opens, parting the waves.

Two large men enter holding a woman between them. Both dressed in white shirts with beige pants and identification badges that hang around their thick necks. The two men have arms like thighs and broad shoulders, yet they still seem uneasy about this task. Their eyes dance back and forth between Peyton and the woman they hold tight between them.

The woman has dark hair with the tips colored purple.

Colorful tats cover her arms. Flowers and thorns mixed with interesting shapes and the large face of a gray wolf peeking out from under her white T-shirt.

She's gorgeous and terrifying.

Eyes like a funeral.

They sit Lady Brubaker down on a stool across the imperfect cherrywood table from Peyton.

Her hands are bound in front of her. The men

lock her chained feet to hooks in the floor. A padded strap is placed around her neck and then secured by a chain to a hook behind her. There's a little slack—so the illusion of conversation has a chance—but this woman with the funeral gaze will not be going far.

People will be watching every angle from outside the room as well, but they know these security measures are more than necessary. Too careful is not a thing. Brubaker has proven to be more than a difficult subject. Actually, she's been tagged as one of the most dangerous people on the planet.

There's a round metallic device imbedded into her forearm.

"Don't bother with the devil tattoos?" Brubaker eyes the silver circle.

"Didn't think we needed to hide things." Peyton forces a smile.

"Not anymore, at least."

Peyton's hands begin to shake. She holds them together by locking her fingers tight.

Brubaker does the same, only without the shaking. Waves roll around them as they look each other over. Peyton wants to let her talk. Forcing a conversational structure on Brubaker won't work. She'll play with you, dance a bit, then slam the door shut and it'll take weeks to crack it back open.

"This is nice." Brubaker looks around the room. "Lovely, actually. Any chance I can be moved in here?"

"Any chance you'll stop putting my people in the hospital?"

"Not much of one."

"Then, no."

Brubaker nods, jamming her tongue in her cheek.

Peyton knew there would be some sparring between them. Both need to circle one another. Assess all the data given from the opponent. Prod and poke for weaknesses. Assess that new data. Then repeat until a level of comfort is reached or until Brubaker shuts down completely.

"Well, Dr. Peyton, you got me out of bed. How can I help you?"

"How are you feeling? I mean with the new treatments."

"Splendid."

Peyton now jams her tongue in her cheek.

"No, really. I feel good. Whatever toxic shit you're pumping through my body and mind is working marvelous miracles. I want to fuck a puppy, then go to church."

"Are you having fun?"

"No." Brubaker slams her hands down on the

table. The chain pulls on her neck tighter. Her veins plump. Violent in a snap. "Not enjoying myself at all, Dr. Peyton."

Peyton's eyes dart to the wall behind Brubaker. She told the men to wait for her word before coming in, no matter what. But given that Brubaker almost killed three agents just days ago, she'd understand if the boys get a little jumpy and storm in on instinct.

"You give, I give." Peyton leans in. Never allowing her fear to show. "If we can open up a dialogue, one like nice, friendly, well-balanced members of society do, then you get things. Nice things."

"Like a puppy to fuck."

"Not helping yourself."

"I want to open up your skull."

"See? This is precisely why you can't have nice things."

Brubaker's fingers dig into the cherry wood.

Peyton leans in closer. They told her to take it easy with Brubaker, but Peyton is tired of dicking around with this woman. She tosses aside the idea of letting Brubaker drive the conversation. Aggression is the only language she seems to respond to.

"Where are the rest of them?"

"I don't know what you're talking about."

Brubaker smiles huge. "I'm all alone in the world. You geniuses made sure of that."

Peyton's teeth grind under her smile.

"Well, I'm never really truly alone. Am I, Dr. Peyton?" Brubaker pokes at her temple with her bound hands. "It's me and Kate in here forever and ever."

Brubaker giggles. Waves crash behind her.

Peyton takes a beat. Slows her roll.

"Do you still feel a difference?" Peyton leans back. So does Brubaker. "Can you tell when there's a shift between Brubaker and Kate?"

Brubaker picks at a knot in the wood of the table. She's shutting down.

"Come on." Peyton considers, then casually flips her wrist in the air, signaling the people outside. "We've got nothing but time. Might as well make the most of it. Let me help."

One of the large men enters holding a silver tray that contains a bottle of high-end bourbon—the good stuff—with two crystal glasses. He sets the tray down in front of Peyton.

"You, meaning Kate, used to enjoy a good stiff drink. Used to work in a restaurant, right? With your husband. Noah, was it? He was a bartender? You two would share a drink at the end of your shifts."

"Stop. You know damn well—"

"The files on Brubaker and Kate are gone. You and your people destroyed them during the escape, but I had another group do a deep dive and found out a lot about you. Both of you." She pours one glass about a half inch. Just a taste. "I'm going to just call you Brubaker from now on. It's easier. Since you're all alone in the world now anyway. Right?"

Peyton pushes the glass toward Brubaker, being careful not to get too close.

"Bit of a light pour, Dr. Peyton."

"Again. You give, I give."

Brubaker looks behind her. The restraints dig into her skin as she looks toward the hidden door where the large man exited.

"What else you got back there?" Brubaker turns back, picking up the glass.

"Anything and everything." Peyton sips her drink. "This doesn't have to be awful. This isn't prison. I know you know how that world works."

Brubaker drinks slow from the glass. Lets it coat her tongue. Closes her eyes as it slips down her throat. A *damn, that's good* expression spreads across her face.

"This?" Peyton circles her finger around the room. "All this is about us learning about you."

"Bullshit. This is about you unpacking your project. About you planting a flag, making a name for yourself."

Peyton thinks about arguing the point but decides not to.

"Probably. Maybe. Yeah, why not. I've worked hard."

"That you have."

"With that understood, I need to know about your friends. They are dangerous people, Lady Brubaker. They are not, as far as I know, sitting in nice ocean rooms sipping expensive bourbon. They're still out there, aren't they? Roaming free with innocent people."

Brubaker shrugs.

"How many are there?"

Brubaker points inside her glass, making a fat lip, begging for a refill.

Peyton shakes her head no.

"Two? Twenty? How many of your loyal subjects are out there? I know they follow you. It's impressive what you've done."

"Thank you."

"Where are they?"

Brubaker only stares back.

"Come on." Peyton waves the bottle. "What

are you holding on to? I can offer you a real life. We can help you."

"There's more like me out there." Brubaker clucks her tongue. "That much is true."

"Okay."

"One more. One, like me."

"Only one?" Peyton shifts. "Where?"

Brubaker's smile is cold. Eyes go dark.

"Where are my children?" Brubaker's face shifts to a new shade of red. "Where are my girls, you fucking piece of shit?" She pounds her bound hands on the table. "Where!"

Her rage is immediate. Zero to a hundred in a blink.

The steel cuts into Brubaker's wrists. Blood drips.

"I'm sorry. We were friends for a second there, right? We were talking nice before I got all crazy. What were we—oh yes, you had questions about the people I may or may not know." Brubaker goes calm, as if a button was pressed inside her mind. "You have no idea, do you? None."

"What—" Peyton stops. Words robbed from her lips.

There's an undeniable change in Brubaker. As if Peyton can see inside her. Her eyes have become clear windows with a breathtaking view of her pain. Brubaker's eyes fill with tears begging to fall. She will not allow them their release. *Is this her? Is this Kate talking?* Her chin quivers as she speaks.

"You have no idea what it's like in here." Brubaker's voice cracks.

"Help me."

"The thoughts she has."

"Help me to understand."

"The memories of the things she's done."

"Kate," Peyton yells. "Talk to me, please."

Brubaker smashes the glass on the wood. Peyton shoves herself away from the table, waving her arms wide for all outside the room to see. Brubaker picks up a sharp chunk of glass.

The large men fly in.

Agent Irving follows.

Brubaker jams the sharp glass into the side of her neck. Peyton dives across the table, grabbing her arm, stopping her from dragging the edge completely across her throat.

Their faces are an inch apart.

Brubaker is strong. Peyton's body shakes while trying to hold her back from finishing the job. Blood drips down onto the cherry wood.

Brubaker's smile is wide. Eyes lost.

"Get her out," Agent Irving yells.

Brubaker is pulled out of her chair. The chunk

of glass clinks to the floor. The large men move her quickly out of the room. Agent Irving barks orders into his comms as he follows.

The door shuts.

The waves roll.

Peyton exhales. Fights to hold back the tremors taking control over her body. She knew having a drink was a risk. She had to try something. *Right?* This wasn't a standard meeting. Not a textbook situation. Having a drink had worked in the past. Worked with Murphy, to some degree. Peyton had to recreate the memory. Had to use the same bourbon, the same style of glasses or it wouldn't take hold inside Brubaker's mind. Anything less would have had a layer of falsehood to it. Authenticity was mandatory. At least that's what Peyton tells herself.

Peyton looks to the smear of blood that stretches from the table to the door. There was nothing in Brubaker's profile that suggested potential suicide. Exactly the opposite. Lady Brubaker has consistently displayed a style of narcissistic personality that would never consider taking her own life. Something is changing in her.

Is her mind changing?

With any scientific endeavor there are starts and stops. Successes and multiple failures. This project was rushed. Not allowed to be tested or perfected as it was intended to be. Not with the Brubaker side or with Murphy.

Peyton's mind flashes to when they first approached Murphy in prison. When he agreed to have his mind altered in hopes of being better. That day, her so-called partner, Agent Thompson, made some cracks about Murphy's mother. Murphy pulled on his steel restraints until his blood spilled. His rage was as sudden as Brubaker's was moments ago.

Peyton downs her drink with a shaky hand.

The door opens up. Peyton nearly jumps out of her skin.

Agent Margo Darby walks in.

Peyton fights not to stand up straight. Something about this woman makes Peyton think she's still in grade school. Makes her feel as if she's always wrong. Darby moves like a shark. Eyes forward yet scanning constantly. Margo Darby is in her early forties, triathlon-fit with shoulders always squared, like she's perpetually prepared for conflict. Face unreadable. After Central Park and Montauk, the CIA put her in charge of this operation. And for good reason.

Darby reaches for the bottle with eyes wide,

looking to Peyton as if asking if she can have a taste of the good stuff as well.

Peyton nods, wrapping her face in hands.

"Well." Darby takes a pull from the bottle. "That went well."

CHAPTER 6

Tomorrow is the day.

A special day for Mr. Madness—formerly nice, quiet Cody Higgins—because tomorrow he will go to the safe house. Tomorrow he will see her. Talk to her. Hear the new plan from Brubaker's lips. Excitement buzzes like a hive inside of him. This is everything. This amazing new life of his is moving forward. Moving forward with the new personality he's really digging deep into, and now he's not far from receiving word from the most important person in his life.

He thought he might feel differently after seeing Murphy in Central Park.

Thought it might change something inside of him.

But it didn't. Still, it's Brubaker he holds as

everything. She's the one who made him who he is. Corrected him. Made him better. Sure, the doctors and scientists *made* him in the clinical sense. They manipulated his mind. Fed him the drugs. Deprived him of sleep, cut skin and bone, worming their way into his skull until he was part Murphy and, to a much lesser degree, part nice, quiet Cody Higgins.

But it was Brubaker who taught him how to live.

How to see the world and everything in it through new eyes. She showed him how to carve through the fog, be better, and how to work the machinery of this new, wonderous life. What a remarkable gift she's given him.

They took Cody Higgins from a discount short-term parking lot near the airport.

It was late at night. Just after midnight, if memory serves.

They kept him for days. His wife barely noticed. Boy is she noticing him now. She's probably telling the police all about him at this very moment. About how her nice, quiet husband killed her boy toy and then put a bullet in one of the thighs she spreads so easily for him. When she tells the story, she'd better call him Mr. Madness.

The least she could fucking do.

"Tomorrow is going to be amazing," Mr. Madness whispers to himself as he grips the leather steering wheel of his dead neighbor's car. Mr. Madness used to lust over this car much in the same way his neighbor used to lust over his wife. Seemed only fair to kill him for what he was doing with his wife and then take this oh-so-fine car for a spin. A black Mercedes pampered and babied to maintain its amazing condition. One that has the option to select autonomous or choose to manually drive, the way free humans who were born to roam do. Also, a car the police will be tracking once they notice it's missing. They will be here soon, of course. That was part of the plan, actually.

Mr. Madness steps out of the car holding an axe.

He took it from the neighbor's garage right before he took the car.

His feet crunch and then squish the grass as he moves up the lawn of his boss's home. His gun is tucked behind his back. He thought the axe would be more of a bombastic touch. A real classic slasher movie sort of feel to what he's trying to accomplish here. The moonlight even catches the blade just right as he stalks toward the front door.

Perfect.

His boss used to love to talk down to Cody.

Dismissed his ideas. Disregarded his contributions on a regular basis. Diminished everything about him. A man who really enjoyed taking out his own insecurities on nice, quiet Cody. Mr. Madness has a little time to kill before his special day tomorrow.

Mr. Madness kicks in the door.

The boss stands a few feet off the living room talking to his wife, who's seated in the colonial living room. His eyes pop wide as plates, freezing upon recognition of who is standing in front of him wielding an axe. Mr. Madness wastes none of his precious time with speeches. No need. He raises the axe up high over his head, then plants the blade into his former boss's chest.

Blood spits and spills.

A spray zip-streaks across Mr. Madness's forehead as he pushes the axe harder into his chest. The boss chokes on his words as they catch inside his throat. He coughs twice, then slumps down to the floor, folding like a dish towel. Mr. Madness keeps his hands gripped tight on the handle. The vibration still working through his arms.

The wife sits on the couch trembling with her mouth open wide, still clutching a glass of wine. She's a much younger woman. A former assistant, if he remembers correctly. Left his second wife for a younger woman. The boss always was a bit of a cliché.

Mr. Madness brushes his hair back.

Thinks he'll shave it later. No, buzz cut. High and tight.

"The company's life insurance is generous. More than likely they will pay out his full bonus, his vested shares, along with six to ten months' salary." He looks her over. "This is the best day of your life. Do better."

He lets go of the handle. Sirens wail outside. They must have finally tracked the car.

"Could I ask for a favor?" The corner of his mouth lifts in a half grin as he pushes his chin toward the street. "Please tell them Mr. Madness did this."

Something buzzes in his pocket.

Puzzled, he removes a phone that is not his. He's never seen it before. No idea how it got inside his coat pocket. Rushing toward the back of the house, needing to exit quickly, he passes by what would have been a lovely dinner cooking in the couple's gourmet kitchen. Smells amazing. His eyes scan the message that appears across the screen of the phone.

You've done good. Do more. Kill everyone at...

There's an address on the screen that Mr.

Madness doesn't know. It's not too far from where he is, but not necessarily close either. He pushes out the back door into the yard, rushing toward the fence. His eyes read over the last line of the text.

Look forward to seeing you at the safe house.

The words vanish from the screen, dissolving into digital oblivion. Time-bomb texts have come into vogue over the years. Texts that leave no trace. His wife and neighbor used them. The screen recognizes your eyes have seen the message, then removes the evidence after a decided-upon time. Usually seconds.

Mr. Madness pulls and lifts himself up and over the fence. His feet land. He picks up speed, running into the dark woods that line a private golf course.

Is this Brubaker contacting him?

Could it be?

Maybe she had to change security protocols with a new phone?

His stomach tingles, delighted by the possibilities.

Of being chosen once again.

Please let it be her.

Tinker and Hiro sit at a strip joint.

They enjoy a drink and don't hate the sights either.

Neither of them were ever strip-joint kind of guys before the big change. That massive change in their brains that linked them with a highly skilled killer named Murphy. Tinker vaguely recalls going to a place like this for a buddy's bachelor party, although he feels like he's been around this side of life more than he clearly remembers.

This might be Hiro's first.

Or this could be one of many.

He too has some cloudy memories. Recalls many bars around the world with women removing their clothes for money. He protected a lot of wealthy people. They could have dragged him into places like this. But that's not it. The flickers of memories are mostly from meeting informants or contacts for jobs, but none of the memories feel like his. The memories, much like Tinker's, feel as if they must be part of Murphy's side of the mind.

"Murphy's done a lot of things," Tinker says, "hasn't he?"

Hiro nods.

They've never talked much about what has happened to them. The combining of minds. The addition of Murphy. Brubaker told them all they need to know.

"Everything has happened so damn fast." Tinker drinks.

Hiro nods, then drinks.

The music thumps a techno anthem from hell. Tinker motions for another drink. The glossy-eyed synthetic bartender stares back at him with the fakest of smiles, then moves toward the cooler stacked with beer in a slight herky-jerky motion. The robotics are better than they were a few years ago but they still lack a true human quality. Tinker guesses the owner was looking to cut back and needed real human women more than a flesh-and-blood bartender.

Tinker used to love a good bar. Used to absolutely adore the drink.

They grabbed Tinker after a meeting at a church. He was sixty days sober. Instead of receiving a celebratory chip, he got to share his brain with a psycho. Tinker isn't sure which he likes better: drinking as a killer, or fighting for a relentless life of sobriety.

Tinker takes a drink.

He likes Hiro. They bonded after the escape. Not sure why. Maybe their pre-Murphy personalities mix well. Hiro rarely speaks but his actions boom louder than hell. They'd kill for one another. They follow the word of Brubaker, but they still have questions, not like some of the others that blindly follow her without thought.

The Murphy addition of crazy hangs on Tinker and Hiro just as heavy as the others, but they have managed to cling on to some healthy skepticism. Maybe they were the questioning type of people before Murphy was jammed into their skulls. Neither Hiro nor Tinker knows for sure. What they do know is that they are free, crazy killers, and they are sitting in a strip joint waiting for a meeting at a safe house that will take place tomorrow.

A drunk guy stumbles over, bumping into Tinker almost knocking him off his stool.

Tinker reaches behind his back, a blink away from pulling his gun. Hiro stops him by grabbing and squeezing his elbow. The drunk slips off, creeping into the smoke of the crowd and out of sight before Tinker can lay into him.

"Asshole." Tinker turns back to the bar, throwing back his chilled vodka.

Hiro nods, confirming, then snatches a cherry from behind the bar.

Tinker's jacket buzzes.

He looks to Hiro. Hiro shrugs. Reaching into his pocket, Tinker finds a phone. One that is not his. Never seen it before. The screen lights up. Tinker and Hiro's eyes scan over a message sent from an unknown source.

A message giving them an address along with orders to kill two men at a hotel.

The time-bomb words dissolve.

CHAPTER 7

GUNSHOTS BOOM.

Muted, but the force is still felt.

A metallic crack of thunder kept under wraps by high-end protective noise-cancelling earplugs. Red's House of Pop & Pow is a small-town gun range but they've stayed up on all the latest in tech. These tiny earplugs are a far cry from the bulky can-like headphones Mother remembers from back in the day. These little babies cancel out the noise that might damage the eardrums but still leave you with the satisfying, clapping crack of power.

Mother learned to shoot in the woods in Texas.

She learned her way around a trigger by taking out innocent beer cans that Father drained moments before. He'd drink 'em dry, toss 'em in the creek, then give her some vague form of instruction as far as how to properly handle a firearm. A fond memory she still holds dear. He disappeared shortly after that, but she never discusses any of that. Not with Murphy. Not with anyone. She just does the pop and pow proper like the old man taught her to.

Murphy chose Red's House of Pop & Pow as the first stop for some quick anxiety relief.

He promised they'd resume their pursuit of the perfect slice of pie after this. Talking with Mother is always difficult—to put it mildly—but it has been nicer. Improved greatly since he picked her up from prison. Murphy guesses that makes some sort of sense. Hard to believe he's thinking this way, but even he has to acknowledge it hasn't been too bad having her around. Up to a point. Murphy realizes the other, newer half of him is more than likely responsible for this fresh view of time spent with Mother.

The scars from when he was young are still healing.

Wounds from the blending of minds run deep and wide.

The balance is still tricky.

Dr. Peyton told him it would be. She talked about the *rough roads* ahead. Told him about the crushing anxiety he would more than likely have to deal with as she gave him multiple bottles of meds, a handful of other scripts to be filled later, and a direct line to her 24/7 if he ever needed her.

Talking will help, she said.

He'd nodded in agreement at the time, knowing he would never dial her up, no matter how bad it got. And Murphy has no desire to call her now. Way too early. He'd like to think he can make it a month or two without running to Peyton with every little blip in his fragile state. But too much time with Mother can spike anxiety like nothing else on God's green earth.

Murphy squeezes the trigger.

Feels amazing.

Been days since he stormed the house in Montauk. Since he fought with the versions of himself, leaving a bloody mess for others to deal with. Blood and bone scattered wall to wall inside that multimillion-dollar home near the water.

Mother stands two "patriot warrior stations" down from Murphy, blasting at a rapid pace using a new Sig. The slick, black metal gleams under the LED lighting. She's using the new Dragon rounds Red recommended the *pretty lady* should use. Mother considered choking the fat bastard out but listened to his pitch anyway. When fired, the rounds give off red and orange swirls of smoke and light that follow the bullet until it reaches its target, giving the so-so illusion of dragon fire.

Murphy uses his trusted Glock. His old friend. The tiny pinhole of light on his sights glows green. Biorecognition still recognizes Murphy as Murphy. This comforts him on some level.

Green means go.

Murphy pushes the button next to him, switching out the targets. An old-time paper target with an outline of a faceless man holding a gun moves silently toward him, gliding along a seamless track in the ceiling. He rips it down, letting it drop to the floor. A new target drops down from the ceiling and returns to the other side of the range.

Murphy reloads.

Mother takes aim at her target, unloading a few quick dragon blasts.

She smiles. Still got it. It's been a while since she pulled the trigger but it's still there. They don't allow a lot of access to guns in prison. Well, none, actually, but she never really thought about it long enough to miss it. Always been somewhat indifferent to guns. Saw them as necessary, at times, but she doesn't long for them as some do.

Mother glances over to her son.

Her *whatever he is now,* she thinks. What's happened to him is a lot to take in. A ton to accept.

Not sure she gets it all, but she does believe him. She sees the change. The difference in him isn't night and day but it's unmistakable. A mother knows when there's a change in her son. She's heard parts of things he's said in his sleep too.

Pressing down the button, the target draws to her, running along its track. Pride rises up inside of her as she inspects her fine work. Two in the chest, one in the neck, and one somewhere north of the faceless man's head.

Murphy blasts away. Rapid. Without pause.

He's in another place. Mind and body are not sharing the same location. Mother watches the intensity. She's seen it before. Saw it at a beach house in California, just before the feds took them both away to prison. There's a lot of baggage between them, to put it mildly, but they're here now. Free folks out shooting guns, eating pie, and rolling across the countryside in a cherry red Porsche 911. Not too shabby. Not at all.

She pulls down the target.

"Well, look at that." Showing it off to Murphy. "Who's the badass in the family?"

Murphy doesn't answer.

Doesn't even glance her way. He's a billion miles away. Thoughts pull and tear inside his healing mind, as if a chain was pulled, opening up the cage door of his rampaging recollections. Everything pouring in, flooding into his mind's eye. He jams his hand down on the steel counter, bracing himself.

"Hey." Mother watches him. "You okay?"

Murphy's fingers press on the cool surface as if trying to poke holes into the steel to hold on to.

"You in there?"

Murphy's teeth grind.

"I'm talking to you." Mother gives him a shove.

Murphy jolts loose from his strangle-trance. Shakes his head. Mother shoves her target into his face, showing off her efforts.

"Yeah? Like that shit?" She smiles huge, seeing the light return to his eyes. "Nice, right?"

Murphy cracks the slightest of smiles. He nods, ejecting the magazine of his Glock, letting it drop clanging off the steel counter. He checks the chamber, then motions to the unseen cameras he knows are there. The door buzzes open. Murphy exits.

"Really?" Mother holds her arms out in frustration. "We're leaving, I guess?"

Mother looks to Murphy's target.

The target's head has all but been removed, hanging on to the track by a shred of paper. Carved off by well-placed bullets. There's also a single shot that stands out.

A gaping hole to the crotch.

Mother is fairly sure her son took the balls first.

Murphy cuts down the street.

His mind a synaptic bonfire. He was better. Felt so much better than he had before. The past was drifting farther and farther away. Where it belongs. But digging into the dirt of his mind has unearthed some wriggly worms. His hands begin to shake. He shakes them back. Opening one of his bottles of pills, he dry swallows one of the reds. Thinks of Dr. Peyton. She'd know what to tell him. He doesn't want to hear it.

He feels Mother behind him as he moves down the street.

Hopes it's Mother behind him.

Mr. Nice Guy is no help right now. None. Murphy used to be able to blame the holes in his psyche on him. Mr. Nice Guy was a wonderful catchall for the troubles of his mind. Now, he's in the same mental soup as Murphy. They are one now. Same mix. Same mess. Not long ago there was a gap—more like a chasm—between them, but today there is little to no line that separates them.

Unstable together.

"Where we headed, tough guy?" Mother calls out, huffing with her cigarette-abused lungs being pushed harder than they are used to.

Murphy shoves open the door to the gym that caught his eye on the way into town.

A rusted metal bell clanks as he storms in like he owns the place.

This small town has been stuck in a time warp of sorts. Nice to see, actually. This red brick gym is no exception. Murphy half-expects to see gray sweatpants and people beating on sides of beef. He made note of every business as they drove in. Took note of the cars in the parking lots. Looking for abnormalities. Seeking the things that might not match up. Things that might tell him if there was someone or something out of place. If there were forces here that might do him and Mother harm.

That, and keeping his eyes peeled for the world's best slice of pie.

The gym has a pulse. The air has a feel to it, along with the stink of sweat and aggression. A lot has changed over the years. Equipment has improved. So have styles of exercise, along with nutrition and the pharmaceuticals of vanity, but one thing still holds true—boxing is still a hand-to-hand thing.

This is classic boxing. Not to be mistaken for the newer, zero-rules fighting style that has all but taken over the betting and entertainment world. This new age of controlled combat doesn't allow for guns or knives, but blunt objects have recently been allowed. Death isn't marketed as part of the entertainment, but fighters have died in the past and others will die in the future. No, what is being taught and practiced here in this gym is the "sweet science," as it was once known. It's making a comeback, from what Murphy has heard. Boxing in its purest form is rising in popularity. As most nostalgia eventually does.

That is what stood out to Murphy.

An old-school boxing gym in today's modern world. There's not a single screen in here. No real sign of tech. He doesn't even see anyone on a phone. The flap of gloves pounding heavy bags, the dull pop of punches landing, provides a rhythm to the place.

Murphy smiles big.

The meat of his mind scratches at a memory. One of him in a ring in Singapore. More like a dirty alley surrounded by a ring of people waving cash and shouting for someone to kick the shit out of him. The simplicity of the fight is what Murphy loved. The results were immediate, and they were not up for debate. The taste of blood. The hurt. The adrenaline spikes. It was all there.

It's here now too.

There are two rings being used. Fighters circle around one another throwing heavy punches and testing lighter ones as well. Bags and equipment are scattered around the available open area. One ring is livelier than the other, however. There's a medium-build man cut from stone with fast hands playing some poor sap like a set of skin drums. The poor sap's head snaps back with each stick of a jab. His body caves with each quick fist planting itself into his body. He's mercifully dropped to the mat with a left hook Murphy saw coming a mile away.

Mother looks around the place.

Enjoys the beef show. The sweat dripping, sliding down the ripples of young muscles. It's a helluva view, to be sure, but she's more concerned with the look that's returned to her boy's eyes.

"You want to work off some of that pie, I get it, but maybe we can go for a walk in a park later."

"Hey," Murphy barks to the young fighter left standing. "You looking for some more work?"

The fighter looks him up and down with a dismissive smirk, then turns away from him. Murphy spreads the ropes, climbing into the ring.

Mother closes her eyes, shakes her head.

No. No. No.

An older man moves up quick on Murphy, putting a hand on his chest. Murphy's heart pounds with excitement. The first spark of conflict he's had in a while. Murphy holds his hands up, signaling he meant no harm.

"Just been on a long drive, friend. Traveling, ya know?" Murphy says with a smile. "Wanted to let off some steam. Maybe help you keep your boy here warm."

"You fight?" the older man asks, looking him up and down. "You don't seem the sort."

"Oh, I fight."

"You get hurt, I get sued into dust—not cool, brutha."

"Not to worry. Got no interest in anything like that." Murphy looks past the older man to the fighter. "He's good, but my bet is that I'm better."

"Let's do this," the fighter says, now interested. Interested in shutting him up. "Let him go."

"Murphy?" Mother raises a hand, as if she had a question at a seminar.

"We'll leave in a moment, Mother."

The fighter's friends snicker.

"He won't be long, little mama," the fighter says. "Might want to call someone to help you carry his body out."

"Bitch, I'll tune you up myself." Mother starts to climb into the ring.

Murphy puts up his hand with his eyebrows raised, requesting her to please stand down. Steam is almost visible rolling out from her ears, but she agrees.

Removing his shirt, Murphy reveals the tats and scars that decorate his body.

He fights the urge to touch one scar in particular. One he got from a stab wound delivered by a loved one. Well, the one he got at a resort in Iraq, care of Lady Brubaker. The violent act was oddly mixed with a loving one. He thinks of a bar he used to work at. A favorite memory. Mr. Nice Guy's favorite memory of him and his wife sharing a drink. Something shifts inside him. An unwelcome slide in emotion.

"Hey." The fighter pounds his gloves together. "We gonna go or no?"

The older man holds some gloves out for Murphy to put on.

His eyes gloss over as he stares down at the gloves. Thoughts adrift. It's been days since he thought about her. About Brubaker and the other woman's mind that's buried deep inside hers. The mind of the woman he loves so dearly.

"What the hell, man? We doing this or what?"

the fighter chirps. "Second thoughts? Not feeling so strong now?"

Mother sees the shift in her son. Fights the urge to call out to him.

Murphy looks at the fighter. At his silly little grin. Murphy's mind whips another direction.

He slips on the gloves.

Cracks his neck. Nods, waving the fighter on. The older man steps aside, shaking his head as he exits the ring. Mother watches. The other people from the gym now gather around the ring. Whispers made back and forth. Money exchanges betting hands. The buzz that filled the gym seconds ago has all but disappeared. The only sound now is Murphy and the fighter.

They circle, sizing one another up. Murphy thinks of the two hundred ways he can snap this guy's bones. Ways to make him beg. Thinks of how he can kill everyone in the gym, burn the bodies, and be on the road before pie time.

Murphy jabs.

The fighter's neck pops back. He didn't even see the punch until Murphy's fist returned home. The fighter shakes it off, considers it lucky. Murphy tags him again. Then again. The fighter returns with a jab and cross. Both find nothing but open air.

Mother grins. Reminds her of when he was a boy. Kicking the shit out of neighborhood bullies who thought they were tougher than tough. Murphy was the tough kid. Made mean by his world. Later, trained by the best of the best.

Murphy punches, weaves, thumps the ribs of his opponent, then breaks his nose with a thundering right. Blood pours from the fighter's nose. Murphy stops. Blood also trickles down from a cut below the fighter's right eye.

Murphy remembers the bleeding from his own eyes.

The hotel room in Bagdad. The alley in New York. The blood tears that would roll down from his eyes without warning. A symptom, he was told, from the mixing of his minds.

Murphy lowers his gloves slightly, a lost expression on his face as his eyes connect with the fighter. His body frozen.

The fighter seizes the opportunity, throwing a lightning-fast jab tagging Murphy's jaw. Murphy cracks a grin. Takes another punch, feeling the slosh inside his skull. These jolts of pain feel like an escape. A sweet form of release.

Murphy mouths the words, *do it.*

The fighter takes a step back, confusion spreading.

Murphy takes a slow, half-hearted swing, missing his target wildly.

Mother looks on. *What the hell is he doing?*

"Drop this clown," she barks with arms wide.

The fighter steps in, unleashing a furious flurry of punches. Building confidence with each flap of glove on skin. Murphy takes it all. Accepting, absorbing the blows one by one. Taking them in like oxygen. His body jerks left and right. Neck whips. Blood drips. Pulsing, swelling skin as a relaxed smile spreads wide.

He is the reason the CIA has Brubaker now.

Murphy set her up to be captured in the middle of that street in New York City. He set up the mother of his children. How could he do that? To her? To his family?

"Hit me as hard as you can," he begs.

The fighter sticks him with a crunching right.

"Harder."

Another right.

"That it? Tell me you can do better. Come on!"

The fighter looks for the knockout.

"Murphy, dammit," Mother screams. "Snap out of it and finish that sack of shit."

Murphy pushes away the sound of her like ignoring a bug near his ear. His guard is nonexistent. Hands lowered. Not even pretending to block the assaulting waves rolling in from the fighter's fists. Mother rushes to the side of the ring, slaps her palms down hard on the canvas sounding like a bass drum.

"This *poor me* bullshit ain't okay," she barks. "I want pie. You promised me pie, ya dickhole."

Murphy's eyes drift to hers.

There's unexplainable warmth behind her stare. A kindness that perhaps only he can see. One that doesn't match her words. Maybe one he's never noticed before.

Mother silently mouths the word, *stop*.

Murphy blinks.

Shakes his head hard. He blocks a left hook coming in. Lands a left to the fighter's ribs. The crunch of bone echoes across the gym floor. Murphy steps in, throwing a sledgehammer right that backs the fighter into the ropes. A blitz of jabs and hooks snaps the fighter's face left, then right. The fighter's knees go weak as he slips down, falling between the ropes. The older man rushes into the ring, tries to pull Murphy back. A useless gesture. A switch has flipped inside Murphy. He keeps pounding away until the fighter slides completely out of the ring and down onto the cold concrete floor.

"Enough," Mother calls out.

Murphy stops. Pulls back with gloves raised.

He yanks the gloves from his pulsing hands, letting them bounce off the mat. Pulling a couple of hundreds out from his pocket, he folds them with an apologetic grin, then lays them next to his blood-slick gloves.

Mother holds open the ropes for her son.

"You know," Murphy says, slipping past her, "eighth-best slice of blueberry is a few short miles away."

CHAPTER 8

THEY FOUGHT like hell about it, but ultimately, they agreed on a motel that didn't suck too much.

Mother didn't want anything too nice.

No fancy-ass bullshit.

Murphy wanted something nice as hell. His days as a highly paid CIA problem solver have refined his tastes. He enjoys the spoils of life, and although he grew up with next to nothing, he's grown accustomed to a certain standard of living life. A standard that removing lives from the planet has afforded him. The Mr. Nice Guy side tends to tilt toward Mother's perspective. All he ever needed was a place to lay his head. However, if Mr. Nice Guy was being honest, the fancy-ass hotels are growing on him.

The blueberry pie they had with dinner was pretty good.

Hard to split hairs on something as subjective as this. Extremely difficult to label one pie eighth best, then clearly define what makes another pie seventh best. Good pie is good pie, but ranking things brings in clicks and eyeballs. And what causes people to stare and tap at screens is king. Regulations passed a few years ago attempted to tighten up the wild, wild west of the world wide web. There were half-hearted attempts to clean up the political crap that plagued social media. The removal of some over-the-top conspiracy rants took years. Regardless of all that, the need to promote and gain visibility in order to generate advertising revenue still rules all.

Top ten ways to lose those unwanted pounds. The eight funniest puppy fails of all time. Top twenty child stars and what they look like now. All eyeball cocaine that feeds the addiction of touching glass in search of whatever is missing. Needy eyeballs are what makes the world turn and turn. The Cash Clash may have brought attention to the great divide between rich and poor, but it will fall way short of solving a damn thing.

To Murphy, that's the real tragedy in what Brubaker did.

A lot of bloodshed and pain with zero upside.

Maybe some good will happen at the margins. The subject will be on the tips of everyone's tongues for a while. It will simmer, perhaps boil, then it will fade as things always do. Once things normalize, the world will land somewhere close to how things were before. Maybe slightly closer to the middle. Incremental change, with signs of a gentle erosion perhaps. Maybe. But if history is any guide, things will move at a glacial pace when the people who can actually crank up change aren't motivated to do so.

That part Brubaker had right.

Problem was, her motivations weren't purely about helping the downtrodden. In Murphy's experience, motivations are rarely pure. She wanted her girls back. Her children. Their children. The two daughters that part of Brubaker and part of Murphy shared together.

Murphy stopped her.

He knows he had to. She had lost control. She was going to cause great harm to a great number of people, but that rationalization doesn't stop Murphy's mind from grinding.

The fighter's punches felt good. That fact he cannot, nor will he try to, deny.

Each pounding fist beat away chunks of his

guilt. He betrayed her. His wife. His best friend and the mother of his girls. He knows he did what had to be done, but he hates that he did it.

The motel room door explodes.

A jarring crack. Tiny spikes of wood splinter and fly. Smoke drifts out from the doorway forming dark, stretching fingers scratching at the air. A kill squad wearing gunmetal gray tactical gear storms in with neon green laser lines tracking from assault rifles. Murphy rolls out from his bed, launching himself at them as his feet touch the carpet. The first one's neck snaps with a dull pop. Murphy puts another one on the floor with a flat-hand chop to an unguarded throat. Jams another man's knee in an unnatural direction.

A knife is plunged into Murphy's stomach.

Blood spills between his fingers as he holds the blade. He drops down to the floor. A masked woman all in black stands over him. She leans down inches from his face. She cocks her head birdlike. As if studying him. Looking for something. Murphy's bloody fingers fumble as he raises them up toward her face. He pulls away her mask.

Mr. Nice Guy's wife stares back at him. The kind, decent side of Brubaker.

Her name sticks at the back of Murphy's throat. Unable to release.

"Say it." She taps the tip of his nose with a bloody finger.

He forces out her name. "Kate."

She nods, then drifts into the smoke.

"Wake up."

Murphy jolts awake. He's on the floor. Mother is shaking him back and forth.

"Wake the hell up," Mother calls out, slapping him.

"Okay. Okay." Murphy holds up his hands. "I'm fine."

"Fine? Fairly fucking far from fine."

Murphy pulls himself up off the floor. "Go back to sleep."

"You said her name last night too." Mother can't hide her concern. "You know that?"

"Who?"

"Kate. Is that Mr. Nice Guy's wife? I mean, sorry, is that your wife's name?"

Murphy goes to the bathroom. Splashes some water on his face.

"You can lie to me all you want to. Been doing it most your life. But this thing? This thing you're working through? It ain't done. Not by a damn sight."

"Stop."

"You sneak off here and there. Hell, a few days

ago, you were gone hours without explaining where you went."

Murphy waves her off, dismissing the words she's saying.

"Then you go all shit-ass crazy in your sleep. What am I supposed to think?"

"I told you. It's over. I'm done with it." Murphy wipes his face. Tossing the towel to the floor, he winces from the cuts and bruises he got from the boxing ring. He forces a smile, hoping to shift the subject. "Now, tomorrow we've got the third-best apple and—"

"It ain't done with you." Mother crawls back into her bed and turns over away from him, facing the wall. "That's all I'm saying."

Murphy stands in the dark, letting the silence fill the room.

He rubs the scar on his stomach.

Doesn't realize he's even doing it.

"There's something I want to show you," he says, barely above a whisper.

"What?"

"Tomorrow." Murphy sits on the bed. "Tomorrow there's something you should see."

"YOU ONLY GET A SECOND OR TWO."

Murphy says this to Mother as he climbs out of the candy apple red Porsche 911.

"To do what?"

"Just follow me and you'll see."

"We've been driving all damn day." She crosses her arms. "You won't tell me a damn thing about where we're going. What the hell, man? What in God's name are we doing out in this—"

"I will show you. Please get out of the car, Mother."

"Nope."

"You said you wanted to take a walk in the park."

"No."

"Get your ass out of the damn car."

Murphy slams the car door shut and points to a neighborhood park across the street.

Mother turns, looking to the patch of green nestled near a pond. An outline of New York City lays out along the edges of her vision. She'd been so pissed at her son for not telling her what he wanted her to see that she didn't really process much around her. They are parked in what looks like some random suburb. A place for young families with so-so money but up-and-coming hopes and dreams.

The park is alive with activity.

The sun shines bright with only a kiss of a cool breeze. Kids dangle their bodies and legs while swaying back and forth in new-looking swings. Moms and dads stand around chatting with other moms and dads, clinging to their coffee. Dogs' tongues wag while running on leashes with joggers weaving in and out of all of it.

"Picnic?" She opens the car door, snuffing out her cigarette in the street. "Odd choice, but okay."

Murphy's attention is focused on the park. He waves her on to hurry the hell up. Mother plays along, trotting up to him, giving a wise-ass salute as she reaches his side.

"Try not to make eye contact." His stare is dead ahead.

"With who?"

"Like I said, you only get a second or two, but it's what we have to work with."

"I need you to tell me what in the sweet hell is going—"

"About thirty yards away. Headed toward us." Murphy talks fast, his voice and head low. "Two adults. One male. One female. Woman in a light-blue yoga outfit. Man in a navy-blue hoodie."

"Yeah, I got 'em. Again, what in the sweet hell—"

"Each are pushing a stroller." His voice cracks. His heart pounds.

Mother's expression softens.

"Okay." Her voice is barely above a whisper. "Is that...?"

Murphy nods.

These are the girls.

She and Murphy will be passing by them in mere seconds. Mother fixes her hair. Murphy does the same. He walks a little taller. So does she. The man and woman pay them no mind, all their atten-tion squarely on the babies.

Good, Murphy thinks.

Murphy knows this man and woman extremely well, although they have never met.

His exhaustive background check, along with breaking into their home to try and find any uncovered dirt, gave him confidence in this couple. Enough confidence to choose them to care for the girls.

The strollers have shades pulled up halfway to shield the babies from the sun. Murphy and Mother are facing the man and woman pushing the strollers and moving toward them fast. They will need to pass the strollers and then turn back if they want to steal a quick glance.

"Remember," Murphy speaks into her ear, "look without being seen."

She nods. She holds her breath. So does Murphy.

As they pass the smiling, attractive couple, Murphy and Mother look away. They whip their heads back around a little too fast to be considered playing it cool. As they turn, the babies laugh and smile. Couldn't ask for a better single frame vision. An image that will burn its way into your mind in the best kind of way. This is what they've driven so far to see.

It was beyond worth it.

Murphy freezes. Feet seemingly sink into the

sidewalk as if he stumbled into a three-foot-deep pool of mud. He can't move. He can't help it. Mother stops next to him.

The faces of the little girls are so bright.

Smiling.

Eyes full of life and wonder.

Murphy wants to believe they saw him. He knows they have no idea who he is. He's a man they've never seen before, but inside of him is their father. Murphy's heart fills, pushing beyond capacity, then breaks in two. His eyes lock. In the girls' little hands are tiny purple rubber ducks.

Murphy pumps his fist in triumph.

They got them. He wasn't sure they'd get them.

Mother covers her mouth, looking to her son. Taking in his joy. Maybe someone else would know what to say to him. A better mother would know the right thing to tell him. She doesn't. Still, it doesn't stop the tears from swelling in her eyes.

"Okay," Murphy says.

"Okay." She wipes her eyes one at a time.

"You got the list?"

"List?"

"The pies."

"Of course I do." Mother clears her throat. "Looks like we're not far from a not-too-horrible slice of apple."

"*Not too horrible* it is, then."

Murphy and Mother turn, moving toward the Porsche. They both know they will not talk much during the drive, and that's fine. Murphy steals one more look at the strollers as they move farther and farther away from him.

Mr. Madness scrubs the blood from his forearms.

The soaps foams into a bright shade of pink as he rubs faster and harder.

He did what the time-bomb message had asked him to do before it faded off into digital oblivion.

He killed them all.

The two men in suits are dead. One died from a gunshot wound to the head. A peaceful shot between the eyes. The second one chose to be beaten to death. Both were trying to get in a car after leaving some sort of meeting. At least that's what it looked like to Mr. Madness. There was a light rain, providing a misty element to the events. Mr. Madness couldn't help but think how cinematic it all was. The lights along the street cutting cones of pale yellow into the night. The gentle rain dusting the pavement as if he was cast in some old spy film.

No idea who they were. He can guess, but that's not his role in the world.

He only knows that she asked him to do what he did.

Brubaker sent him a message. He can feel it. Feel her through the digital words. Words that contained orders to do what she needed to be done. She trusted he would act without question, that he would execute orders without need for further explanation. She knew he was the one to ask, that he's moving more toward something special that maybe only she can see. Transforming into something new and wonderful.

Correction.

Changed into what he always wanted to be but was never strong enough to accept until now.

Looking in the mirror, Mr. Madness inspects a small cut on his cheek. Must have come from his tussle with the second one. Scrappy little bastard. Wiry with misleading looks, but he was a fighter. Until he wasn't.

Mr. Madness fixes his hair.

Blood begins to stream down from his right eye. Then a line rolls from his left. With a smile, he wipes them away with the fatty part of the back of his hand. The slick crimson smears give him the appearance of a deranged clown. Mr. Madness likes it—likes it a lot—but he knows this look will not play out in the civilized world. Civilized is not a world Mr. Madness finds any interest in. Not one he would choose to roam.

The meeting at the safe house is coming soon.

Soon, he'll see her again.

Excitement vibrates his entire body.

Hiro threw the man off the balcony.

Not the way Tinker would have gone with this, but what does he care.

The message said to kill this guy at the hotel.

Tinker is glad they got to the room while the man was having dinner. The room service cart still sits by the bed with the silver dome covering whatever meal the man currently falling to his death will never enjoy. A bottle of red wine sits next to it. The man had a little weight on him, so Tinker is guessing whatever is here is pretty good. Smells tasty at least.

Hiro adjusts his jacket while walking over from the balcony. His large frame blocks the moonlight as he moves toward Tinker with curtains rippling in the wind behind him.

Hiro extends his arms, shrugging his shoulders.

"No idea," Tinker says, lifting the silver dome lid. His eyes light up seeing the plate. "Oh, hell yes."

Score.

A massive bacon cheeseburger with what looks like garlic fries spilling over from the plate. Tinker sits on the bed, rolling the cart in position in front of him. Hiro sits on the bed next to him.

"Brubaker?" The first thing Hiro has said in days.

"Maybe. Who the hell else would it be?" Tinker cuts the burger in half, placing half on a napkin for Hiro.

Hiro nods a thanks, then tilts him a look with his eyebrows raised.

"I do know we need go into this safe house tomorrow with eyes open wide." Tinker opens the bottle of red. "Enter with some extreme caution present."

Hiro nods again, takes a massive bite from the burger half.

Tinker fills up the lone wine glass and hands it to Hiro. Hiro picks up a glass, tosses the water out on the floor, then hands it to Tinker so he can pour himself some wine. They chew their burgers and sip their wine in silence.

"You know?" Tinker says with mouth full. "Won't take long to figure out what room that fat ass flew out of."

Hiro nods, sips his wine.

Tinker chews.

"Yeah." Tinker picks up his plate. "Should really take this to-go."

CHAPTER 11

Darby's office is intimidating as hell.

Peyton is certain this is the desired effect.

There's a hint of something in the air. A faint scent that hangs just out of reach from identification. Perhaps like a doctor's office, if Peyton had to label it. A clinical feel to a workspace that is kept in a lab-like spotless condition. Peyton thinks about the care that went into designing the wave room. A room Darby was in charge of creating.

The room where were the conversation with Brubaker went so wrong.

The walls of Margo Darby's office are the color of gunmetal steel, with two pops of color in the form of hanging art displaying shapes and blobs in various shades of blues. Both by an Atlanta artist, if Peyton's memory serves. Circular lights pepper the ceiling above a long, polished, dark wood desk with two chairs positioned in front. Peyton is seated in one of them, shifting, adjusting her jacket that feels ridiculously tight at the moment.

This is the third time she's been in here.

First time was when Darby was put in charge of the mess they are currently in. The mess of Markus Murphy and everything surrounding him. Peyton had never met Darby before, let alone worked with her.

With her, not *for* her.

Work is another word that itches inside Peyton's brain.

This all might be work for Darby, part of her job, just another box to be checked, but not to Peyton. To her, this is far from punching the clock. This is more like her heartbeat. The science she and her team began is her reason for breathing. There is nothing else. She has poured everything she has into this, only to watch it morph into a global catastrophe, and she's had a front row seat to the entire unraveling disaster. A perfect view of everything she's lived and worked for set ablaze before her very eyes.

However, Peyton is a realist.

She knows what is in the past belongs there and the only way forward is through Darby.

Doesn't love it, but it's where she is. Her father used to talk often about living to fight another day. Peyton's edges might be frayed, her nerves on the verge of shattering, but make no mistake, Peyton is alive and prepared to fight as hard and long as it takes.

"Can I get you something?" Darby asks. "Besides a new jacket."

Peyton gives a polite laugh, tugging at her right shoulder. She has found Darby to be a sharp, highly intelligent woman with a dry sense of humor that cuts like a dull knife.

She also doesn't trust her.

Not at all.

Peyton knows this mistrust stems from her past experience with the CIA. Thompson was her past experience. Her only experience. And that was more than enough to formulate her opinion. Thompson was a former CIA agent who moved on to the private side serving as a bridge for new, rising tech and biotech firms that needed a little seed money and would do almost anything to have access to that funding. Funding the CIA could and would gladly provide with unspoken strings attached.

Peyton was one of those rising biotech firms in need of money to seed her life's work. Former CIA agent Thompson was her main point of contact with the agency prior to Murphy blowing his head off.

Thompson lied to Peyton from the very beginning.

Failed to mention there was a separate CIA group mirroring Peyton's work. Stealing, using her research and bleeding-edge science to develop dirty deeds.

Peyton wanted to help people.

Do good with her work by adding balance to troubled minds through advanced medical and psychological treatments after her younger brother died from an overdose, losing his long battle with a lifetime of issues stemming from an extreme bipolar disorder. She created a way of mixing the unstable with the stable for the benefit of everyone.

The CIA wanted the opposite.

They wanted to inject murder into the minds of stable, functional people in order to create on-demand killers. Push-button psychopaths ready and waiting for orders. Lady Brubaker was part of that group. She was a highly trained killer mixed with the mind of a lovely, kind woman named Kate.

Brubaker led others like her in a takeover of the lab where they'd been poked and prodded. The main difference, her followers were all males who had Murphy mixed into their minds. Brubaker was the lone female, which is why Kate was used. Together, Brubaker and her followers rose up and killed everyone in the lab that held them captive. CIA agents, doctors, scientists were all slaughtered. Then, Brubaker and her Murphy-mixed followers vanished into the wind. Became ghosts. Hell had been set loose, until Peyton and Murphy did their best to put a lid on it.

"Shitshow." Darby runs her tongue over her teeth. "*Shitshow*? Would you consider that a tired, yet accurate description of what's going on?"

"Reasonable assessment." Peyton sits up straight.

A corner of Darby's mouth lifts, giving the thinnest of smiles.

"Brubaker is in surgery right now."

"Is she—"

"Gonna die?" Darby lets a little of her Georgia roots slip through. "Lost a lot of blood. Given her skill set, she knew the best place to start the cut, so I really don't know. Bit of a pain in the neck, however."

Peyton smiles at the joke. Not sure if it was one.

"It didn't go well. I acknowledge that." Peyton

clears her throat. "But there wasn't anything in her profile that suggested a risk of suicide."

"Which profile? There's two on her, of course."

"Neither of them. Kate had nothing vaguely signaling suicidal behavior. And Brubaker is a psychopathic narcissist. The studies are mixed, but that mental makeup plus her history does not suggest she would ever consider taking her own life."

"Far more likely to slaughter everyone in the building than kill herself."

"One would think." Peyton clears her throat again. Shoulders inch up like earrings. "I took something I knew from her past, and within reasonable risk parameters, I hoped that I might create an open environment. Get her to—"

"You rolled the dice based on data."

"Yes."

"That's not something you need to apologize for, Dr. Peyton." Darby's eyes drill in. Impossible to read her intentions. "That's something we tend to do around here. Taking reasonable risks to sidestep unbridled hell is plenty cool with me."

Peyton's shoulders lower. Not entirely, but a little.

"They call this the Split-Head Project. Did you know that?"

"What? Wait. Who's *they* exactly?"

"Some wise-ass agent started it. Probably that douche Irving. But the name has some teeth to it. It's caught on around here. The higher-ups are calling it that now too."

"How sensitive of them."

"That former agent you worked with really screwed that whole thing up, didn't he? Thompson was it?"

"He did. Caused a lot of pain for a lot of people."

Darby nods. She turns her chair slightly to the right, looks out the window.

"We've been digging through things. Sifting through the wreckage of what was left when Brubaker and her friends escaped the lab and—"

"Excuse me." Peyton cuts in. Her heartbeat cranks up a few more beats per second. "Do you mind if I stand up? I think better when I'm standing. Moving, actually. More like pacing. I think better when I'm pacing, and this sounds like a conversation where I should be pacing."

"Please do." Darby playfully motions for her to rise.

Peyton stands, beginning to pace back and forth. Darby watches her with that thin smile working overtime.

"I'll cut through most of the shit, Dr. Peyton. We've found there are a few of Brubaker's split heads, for lack of better term, still out there."

"We thought that would be the case."

"True. We did. We still don't know the exact number, and unfortunately, we discovered there are a few more things we didn't know."

Peyton speeds up her pace, thinking of how Brubaker said something about one being out there. One out there being like her. Peyton keeps it to herself, although she knows full well that Margo Darby has reviewed the recordings from her conversation with Brubaker.

"We think someone from the CIA side of that project survived the escape."

"Who?"

"Not completely sure. There are four potential agency personnel unaccounted for and—"

"Four?" Peyton blurts out.

Darby nods, wiggling four fingers with her thumb folded tight into her palm.

"Well..." Darby balls her wiggling fingers into a fist and turns back toward the window. "There's only one who's actually alive now."

Darby taps her desk without looking away from the window. The curtains pull closed as the over-head lights dim. The far wall illuminates, flickering, then shows a photo of a man laid out dead in the street.

Peyton winces a bit at the sight of what happens to the human body after falling from a considerable height.

"This guy fell out of a hotel. And..." Darby taps, then slides her finger along her desk. "These two died in a parking lot. One took a bullet to the head. The other one was beaten to death. All three died last night. All three right around the same time."

Peyton stares at the screen, slows her pacing.

She doesn't recognize any of them, but why would she? She never had any contact with the members of the CIA who stole her work. She didn't know they even existed until recently. Thompson made damn sure of that.

"Who did this?" Peyton asks.

"Not sure. Surprisingly, there is no footage of the parking lot or from the hotel. Not a single security camera or anyone's personal device caught a shot of any of it."

"How is that possible?"

"It's not. Not in today's world."

"You said four survived the lab. This is only three."

"Your math is correct. There's one left. A CIA-sponsored scientist. Much like yourself."

"Nothing like me." Peyton said it with a little more bite than she intended.

"Apologies." Darby resets. "A man named Ernesto. We are still pulling all we know about Dr. Ernesto, but what we do know is that he was on the opposite side of this project from you. Highly respected in the field of neuroscience. Knee-deep in some shadow ops that—"

"He was involved with Brubaker and—"

"And the rest of the ones who escaped? Yes. Ernesto was the main brain on that side."

"Fucking fantastic." Peyton lets the words slip without realizing it.

"What's really fucking fantastic," Darby says with a crack of her knuckles, "is that we can't find him."

"You think this Ernesto killed these people?" Peyton points to the grisly images on the wall while picking up the pace of her pacing.

"I doubt dear Dr. Ernesto did this. He's in his early sixties and is about the size of a schnauzer."

"Then who?"

"We like some of Brubaker's buddies for this."

"What?" Peyton comes to dead stop. "You really think so?"

"We do."

Peyton goes back to pacing, letting her mind work through it.

"You still keep pretty close tabs on Murphy, correct?" Darby asks.

"Of course I do." Peyton studies the photos of the dead. Processing. "You know I do."

"Was that part of the agreement with him?"

"Something like that." Peyton stops, turning to Darby.

Darby nods. Her stare bores through Peyton. Unreadable as hell. "You know, some people in this building think he never should have been let out in the wild."

"Some people haven't seen what I've seen."

"Not saying I'm one of them."

Bullshit, Peyton thinks.

"Do you track him?" Darby lets out a soft chuckle.

"Constantly."

"You trust him?"

"I trust part of him." Peyton starts pacing again.

"He is part scary dude."

Darby taps her desk. The wall goes dark. The curtains open up, letting light creep back into the office. Staring at Peyton for a minute too long, Darby lets the silence pick away at her. Peyton fights everything inside of her not to talk first. She knows this is a game to Darby.

"We need to find Markus Murphy. We need to talk with him."

"We?"

"Well, you. For now, *you*." A veiled threat if ever there was one. "His special level of insight might be valuable at a time like this."

Peyton takes her original seat in front of Darby's desk. The wheels in her mind spin.

"That a problem?" Darby looks back to the window, as if removing herself from the room.

"Murphy is in a fragile state right now."

"Aren't we all."

"I'm being serious."

"I'm not kidding."

"I think there might be something happening chemically. I need to run tests on Brubaker, but her sudden suicide attempt concerns me. On several levels."

"And that concern is?"

"I'm concerned they might be crashing. To put it in blunt terms."

Darby nods without looking her way.

"I don't think—" Peyton stops, resets. "Not sure we should disrupt the healing process that—"

"Not sure I'm asking permission." Darby turns back to Peyton, her thin smile returning.

Peyton leans back, holding on to the arms of the chair. A sudden suffocating feeling grips her. Like icy fingers wrapping around her throat. A sensation she never experienced prior to *working* with these people. And this new working-with-the-CIA choking feeling, it is becoming a little too familiar for her liking.

"Where's Murphy?" Darby asks.

Now Peyton looks out the window. Darby clears her throat, guiding attention back to her.

"Where is he, Dr. Peyton?"

Peyton pauses. Thinks.

"He's eating pie with his mother."

CHAPTER 12

Best pie in the universe.

That's the bold statement on the sign out front.

An impossible claim to prove, but Murphy has noticed that these insane results posted from unnamed competitions are commonplace among the pie-making elite.

Best cheesecake in the state.

Best whatever in the USA.

And now, best pie in the universe.

This slice of pie is pretty damn good, however. Mother hasn't said much since they left the park. Since they made that quick detour stopping to see the girls. Murphy can't imagine what's going through Mother's mind. Trying to pin down her thoughts has always been an amazing act of futility.

She's been many things over the years, but easy to read is not one of them.

Mother chews her bite of pie and sips her coffee.

The diner they're seated in is small but not tiny. The décor is an odd mix of the past and present. There's a picture of Elvis next to a large portrait of the new high-speed rail that rockets people around the East Coast like cattle riding a bullet stuck on a bolt of lightning. There's an ancient pie carousel slow turning the best pie in the universe, along with some of its lesser dessert friends. A rotating glass tube of goodness. The glass projects slow-dissolving, brightly colored names and prices of the desserts on display. Provides a modern touch along with the nostalgia. A smiley face gets mixed in here and there amongst the dollar signs.

Murphy's eyes dart.

Scanning, processing his surroundings constantly.

He can tell you the height and weight of every-one. He knows whether everyone here is right or left-handed, customers and staff included. He's not sure about the kitchen, but his best guess is there are two to four people working back there. He can also safely assume there are three exits to the diner at the minimum. The front door they came in, the window in the men's room—probably one in the women's—and there has to be at least one leading out the back of the kitchen for trash and deliveries. He has enough bullets to kill or immobilize everyone, but he doubts the likelihood of any of them being threats.

One never knows, however.

It's the *never knows* that can and will get you killed.

The threats will more than likely come from outside this diner. His mind churns through this style of analysis in a looping serpentine of data. Taking in the new inputs and stimuli. Process, report, then repeat as needed.

Mr. Nice Guy is melting into this pattern of thinking, adding what he knows about the world into the mix of what Murphy brings to the party. Locations, parts of the country, and perhaps most importantly, people. He knows personalities and types of people better than Murphy, who basically only knows two types of humans—bad people and worse people, and those aren't always easy to spot. Sometimes, often actually, they are one and the same.

"You gonna talk to me about those girls?" Mother finally breaks open the quiet.

"What would you like me to say?"

"Anything would be nice."

"It's a little complicated."

"No shit."

"You saw them." Murphy wipes his mouth with his napkin. "They're better off where they are."

"That why you keep visiting them?" Mother locks her eyes with his. "Sending them ducks and shit? Because you're so damn blessed at letting things go?"

"It's compl—"

"Complicated. Yeah, you said that."

Murphy thinks about his gun again.

Easy.

A familiar woman's voice cuts in.

"Murphy."

Murphy looks up. Dr. Peyton stands a few feet from their table.

"Hi." Murphy hides his surprise.

Surprised isn't supposed to be a thing with Murphy. He can't believe he allowed her to walk into the diner without detection, let alone slide up to their table. He's getting soft. Mother and Mr. Nice Guy Noah are dulling the edge they all need so badly to survive.

"Who the hell are you?" Mother grips her fork like a weapon.

"Peyton." She extends a hand.

Mother doesn't accept the gesture, looking to her son for confirmation.

"Dr. Peyton, actually," he says.

"Oh." Mother recognizes the name. "Dr. fucking Frankenstein—"

"She's okay, Mother. I told you about her."

Peyton motions to the open chair, asking if she can join them. Murphy nods. Mother goes back to her pie keeping her eyes down. Peyton takes a seat as a waitress comes over. While Peyton orders some coffee, Mother fires eyes at Murphy, making her concern known. He raises a hand begging for calm. *Please* in his eyes.

"Happen to be in the neighborhood, Dr. Peyton?" Mother asks.

"Not far." There's a forced smile in Peyton's voice. "I'll pay you the courtesy of not lying. I track your son's movement constantly."

"Ya don't say?" Mother drops her fork. "That's some unconstitutional shit right there."

"I'm also the one who helped get you out of prison."

Mother resets. Murphy can't help but smile.

"So?" Murphy places a hand on his mother's

hand that's tightly gripping the fork again. "Now that we're all friendly, what can we help you with, Dr. Peyton?"

"Like some pie?" Mother says through gnashed teeth.

"There's a potential problem." Peyton mouths a soft *thank you* to the waitress as she drops off her coffee. "A rather ugly, potential problem. You know I wouldn't show up here casually."

Murphy nods.

Peyton would never simply pop in to say howdy. His fingers spread out on the table seeking stability. Attempting to find calm in the storm as Peyton tells them about the scientists who have been murdered. Explains some of what has happened. That these scientists survived the Brubaker escape and there is one more out there. A lead scientist they can't find. She also explains the CIA believes others—followers of Brubaker who share Murphy's mind—are out there roaming the land and they are responsible for the murders of these scientists.

She leaves out the suicide attempt by Brubaker, not knowing the effect that information may have on him. Could potentially be catastrophic. Peyton needs to know more about Murphy's state of mind.

"Split-heads?" Murphy almost chokes on his pie. "That's what they're calling them?"

"Kinda what they're calling you too," Peyton adds, taking a bite of his pie.

"Split-heads." Mother giggles with a mouthful. "That's so great."

Murphy's mind folds in on itself. He's avoided thinking about the escape and the nasty process of minds mixing. Of his mind being added, blended into other people. Innocent civilians who now share his mindset for killing. He's pushed down the idea that the work Peyton did had been stolen, mutated, made ugly, and used on Brubaker and others. He feels himself drifting. As if he's dragging himself away from all that's happening. Pulling himself to safety, away from the twisted wreckage of reality.

"What does any of that have to do with me?" Murphy asks.

"Is that a serious question?" Peyton asks.

"Felt like a serious question."

"They are part you, Murphy. You are part them, and they are starting something. No idea what exactly. Seems like they're working with, or maybe attempting to find, this Ernesto. We don't know for certain."

"We?" Murphy says, putting his hand up. "You full-blown CIA now?"

"No." Peyton wants to avoid him baiting her into a fight. "Work with, not for."

Murphy shrugs. *If you say so.*

"Murphy," Peyton continues, "please make no mistake, there is without question something going on and it is not good."

"Sounds just like a job for the big bad CIA."

"Big bad." Mother giggles again.

Peyton glances toward Mother, then back to Murphy.

"You can't act like this has no effect on you."

"Not an act." Murphy signals for the check.

Peyton takes a deep breath.

"Murphy, they sent me here to talk to you." She holds her hands out in front of her as if asking for a reset. "There's someone new in charge of this. Agent Margo Darby. She sent me here to try and convince you to help us."

"There's that word again," Murphy snaps. "You and another agent asked for my *help* not that long ago. You remember any of that?"

"I do."

"Good. So, you will completely understand when I politely request that you tell Agent Margo

Darby and Operation Split-Head to fuck the fuck off."

Murphy tosses some cash on the check, then shoves back hard from the table. The back of the chair bounces off the tile as he walks out the door.

Mother chews her pie. Drinks her coffee.

Peyton stares at the empty space where Murphy sat only seconds ago.

Mother stands up, placing a soft hand on Peyton's shoulder.

"He's talked about you," Mother says. "Said some nice things, actually. Fairly rare for him."

"That's the nice part of him talking."

"Yeah, you're probably right about that." Mother considers. Stops, then says it anyway. "I should probably thank you. Whatever you did worked. Or I should say, is working. He's a mess of biblical proportions, but he's better than he was."

Peyton fights a smile, but she can't fight the warmth spreading through her. The feeling your work did some good is pretty powerful. Even with its flaws. Even after all that's happened.

"Can I ask you something?"

"Depends, Dr. Peyton."

"Is he..." Chooses her words. "Is he having problems?"

"Really?"

"I mean is he having problems with the change?" Peyton tries to lock into her eyes. "It's important. I need to know if you've seen any problems with how he's handling the mental changes."

Mother stares at her. Tries not to show it on her face, but she can't hold it back. She thinks of what she's seen. The nightmares. The firing range. The boxing ring.

With eyes full, Mother gives a single nod.

Peyton nods back, not pressing her for more.

"This isn't over. Is it, Dr. Peyton?"

Peyton picks up a fork, stealing another bite off Murphy's plate. "Not even close."

CHAPTER 13

T H E   S A F E   H O U S E is more like a barn.

"Guess safe barn doesn't sound as cool," Tinker whispers to Hiro.

The vacant farm looks like it was abandoned some time ago. American farming took a nosedive years ago. The few that could survive consolidated, leaving the rest to wither and fade. The moon hangs above, framing the remains of a large, two-story home that looks like it would fall over if you clapped your hands too close to it. Blown-out windows with rags posing as curtains sway in the night breeze. Acres and acres of open land surround the broken-down home with patches of grass peppering the dirt with stubborn blades of brownish-green. A poor showing of the last bit of life that clings to this once-proud farm.

Despite the appearance of the house, the barn is in far better condition.

Its all-metal construction still has some shine to it under the starry night sky. Not in amazing shape, small spots of rust here and there, but unlike the house, the roof at least seems intact.

"Must have been built a couple of years ago. If not sooner." Tinker pushes his chin toward the barn. "Looks less like shit."

Hiro nods.

They circled the area three times.

Arrived here about an hour before the scheduled meet time so they could be sure. Allowed them time to inspect all the angles of the farm and a half-mile radius of the property. Doing what they could to make sure they weren't walking into some sort of bloodbath ambush. Unlikely, considering Lady Brubaker gave them this location, but anything is possible given all that's happened.

Trust but verify.

Tinker and Hiro stand amongst the trees about a hundred yards from the entrance to the barn. A cool wind blows, moving the tree limbs and creating a shadowy dance around them.

Tinker checks his phone.

"It's time."

Hiro nods.

They pull their guns.

Neither one likes the exposure time this is going to require. They will be moving without cover for longer than anyone would consider comfortable. Being out in the open for the amount of time it's going to require for them to get from where they are to the barn is not a strong tactical move. The problem is, there's no other way. The barn is almost exactly in the middle of the open land and where they are standing is the shortest distance to it.

Maybe that was the idea.

This is a smart, safe spot that's been chosen. But safe for whom is the big question. Certainly not for Tinker and Hiro. Brubaker will be able to see them, or whoever, clearly in all directions. No way for anyone to sneak up. She'll be able to react to whatever is coming her way. Brubaker was, and still is, the smartest person in most rooms.

Smart safe barn, indeed.

Tinker and Hiro decide that staying low and moving with purpose is the best and only way to go. Hiro will watch their backs while Tinker scans the area as they move forward. They will be sitting ducks for a full minute, maybe two if the terrain is rougher than expected. They will run hard and shoot first if necessary.

Again, they have no choice.

They talked about not showing up. About just avoiding this meeting altogether. They have some money. They have weapons. Do they really need this meeting? Can't they go and make a life without this? It wasn't a long discussion—meaning Tinker talked and Hiro listened and nodded—but they both agreed they needed to, at the very least, show up to the meeting.

A light flickers from inside the barn.

Tinker stops holding up a fist. Hiro stops cold.

The barn's light peeks through the cracks, giving an eerie strobe to the open field before the light finally stays on. The large steel door rolls open, but no one can be seen clearly inside. Tinker can make out two hints of shadows at the edges.

"I count two inside."

Hiro studies the light inside the barn. Then holds up two fingers, confirming Tinker's assessment. Tinker shakes his head, not liking this one bit.

Hiro doesn't either.

They recheck the loads of their guns, take a deep breath, then continue pushing toward the barn. Only faster now. Tinker moves up to the side of the wide-open door as Hiro takes a position farther back that gives him a clear sight line of the door.

Tinker looks back to Hiro.

Hiro nods, taking aim at the open barn door with a two-handed grip. Tinker raises his gun, deep breath, then spins into the barn.

A single lightbulb hangs down by an orange cord.

Standing under it are two men.

One is calm and cool. Slicked-back hair. Nice suit. Hands stuffed inside his pockets while rocking back and forth on his heels. Tinker has never seen him before. However, the man standing next to him Tinker does recognize. Can't remember his name, but he knows he's one of Brubaker's people.

He's like Tinker and Hiro.

Mr. Madness turns to Tinker, removing his fingers from the gun tucked behind his back.

"You know this man?" Mr. Madness asks Tinker, motioning to the other man.

Tinker breathes slightly easier seeing the recognition in the eyes of Mr. Madness. Calling him a friendly face is a stretch, but at least they know one another. Tinker studies the calm, cool man with olive skin in the nice suit. He shakes his head no, then motions outside for Hiro to join them.

"Irving." Agent Irving offers his hand knowing

Tinker won't shake it. "I was just telling your friend and colleague here that I'm with the CIA."

"Why hello, Agent Irving." Tinker raises his gun, wanting to shoot the smile off Irving's face.

Irving places his hands back in his pockets, never breaking away from cool.

Hiro enters the barn with his aim dead at Irving's head.

Mr. Madness gives Hiro a nod.

"I'm on your side, Tinker. You too, Hiro." Irving gives a toothy smile with a cock to his head. "Please, there's no need for guns and hard words."

"He might be okay." Mr. Madness gives vague validation. "Tell them what you told me, Agent Irving."

"I'm the one who sent those messages," Irving says. "The time-bomb messages."

"You?" Tinker lowers his gun. "Thought those were from her."

Hiro does not lower his weapon.

"Her?" Irving asks, then resets. "Oh, you mean Brubaker. It is her message, but I'm the messenger. I slipped that phone in your pocket at the naked lady joint." Leaning against a rusted-out piece of farm equipment. "Pretty slick, right?"

Tinker remembers the drunk who slammed into him at the bar.

"We needed to see where your heads were at, so to speak. I realize that's a loaded statement if ever there was one."

"You testing us?" Tinker sneers.

"More or less. You all passed, by the way." Agent Irving shrugs. "We really wanted to see what you're capable of out there in the field."

Tinker thumbs between himself and Hiro. "So you had us take out that guy at the hotel?"

"Threw him out a window." Irving laughs. "Literally raining men."

No one shares his laughter. Hiro knows it was a balcony—technically—but lets it go.

"Sorry." Irving cuts his laughter short. "It's an old pop song—"

"We know," Hiro says, regripping his gun. Keeping his aim on Agent Irving's head.

"Wow. Didn't know that one talked." Irving turns to Mr. Madness. "And you. You, we wanted to see if you could rise up and take out two all by your lonesome."

"And I did. Easily." Mr. Madness's stare is blank. "Who were these people you had us kill?"

"Surprised you gents didn't recognize them."

"How's that?" Tinker asks.

"They were scientists who did some work on

your brains." Irving plops a stick of gum in his mouth, then offers the pack to them.

Tinker looks to Hiro. Hiro lowers his gun.

"Where is she?" Mr. Madness asks.

"Who?"

"Brubaker."

"Oh." Special Agent Irving chews. "They've got her locked up."

"You talk to her?" Mr. Madness bites back his excitement.

"Every day."

Mr. Madness feels a flash of heat rush inside of him. There's a tingle to his stomach. He can't place the emotion exactly, but it feels a lot like jealousy. Heat flashes to his face. This man, this Agent Irving, gets to spend time with Brubaker.

"Look, guys." Irving pushes off from the tractor. "We're only trying to continue the good work she started—"

"You keep saying *we*." Tinker's anxious energy rises as he bounces on the balls of his feet. "Who does that include exactly?"

"There's the billion-dollar question." Irving snaps, pointing a finger at Tinker. "You see, a few people barely escaped that massacre at the lab that day." He holds up a hand. "Now, I completely understand why you and your buddies did what you did, mind you. The frustration must have been enormous. But these folks survived the slaughter. So, we gave you an opportunity to finish the job—kind of."

"You keep talking in circles, man." Tinker starts to finger his gun.

Hiro does the same.

Mr. Madness crosses his arms. Wants to hear more.

"You're right. I'll tighten it up. Another doctor. A man of science." Irving holds up an old-school black-and-white photo. "Sorry for the ancient medium, but digital can't really be trusted given the circumstance. CIA has all kinds of fun gadgets."

They all stare at the photo.

It's like the three of them are seeing a ghost.

"Now, do you remember this large-brained man?"

"Ernesto," escapes Mr. Madness's lips.

Agent Irving snaps his fingers again, points to Mr. Madness.

"What is all this?" Tinker asks. "What do you two want?"

"There's more work to be done." Irving sets the photo down. "We can continue. We can expand what Brubaker started."

"Can you get her out?" Mr. Madness can't hide

the schoolboy sound to his voice. "Can we talk to her?"

"I can and you will."

Tinker and Hiro share a look.

"There's a catch. Kind of a big one." Irving bounces his eyebrows. "There are more people that need to go away."

"Who?" Tinker asks.

"One will be a little more challenging than the other."

"Who is it?" Tinker squeezes his fists until his knuckles pop.

"Markus Murphy."

The name hangs in the air.

"You know the gravity of that request?" Mr. Madness asks.

Agent Irving nods.

"Why does Murphy need to go away?" Tinker asks.

"He's the alpha for the other side of the equation." Irving starts to move around the barn. "Murphy is the holder of all the science for them. Without Murphy, the CIA has nothing. They can't crack Brubaker."

Mr. Madness smiles. A flutter in his stomach. She's too strong.

"So, he represents the only research avenue for

them," Irving continues. "They monitor his vitals, his biology, everything about him. They use this data to alter and perfect what they're doing. Sad thing is Murphy doesn't even really know it's happening. Poor bastard thinks he's free." Irving stops, taking a dramatic pause. "As long as he's alive, the CIA will continue their work and keep us from ours."

Tinker, Hiro, and Mr. Madness listen. Something in his words does not ring true.

"And the other person you say needs to go away?" Mr. Madness asks.

"Another scientist. Named Peyton." Irving shows them another photo.

Mr. Madness nods. He remembers seeing Murphy with this woman in Central Park shortly before all hell broke loose.

"There's been a hard-hitting agent assigned to this. Margo Darby. She will not stop until you people—" Irving holds up a hand as if asking for a reset. "Sorry. She will not rest until you fine gentlemen are in the ground. They've already started looking for you."

The three share looks.

"Don't worry. I was obsessively thorough when covering up the mess you created. There was a whole lot of digital footage of you taking the lives of those scientists that needed a good scrubbing. But I can only do so much, and it is only a matter of time before the wrong people start asking the right questions."

"You're full of shit," Tinker says. "You are holding back some serious chunks of information here."

Hiro nods.

"Full transparency on this side of the conversation, my good man."

"Bullshit," Hiro says.

"Always shocked when he speaks." Irving smirks.

"Nope." Tinker raises his gun. "Do not trust you."

Hiro raises his weapon as well.

Agent Irving raises his hands. "Guys, look—"

"No," Mr. Madness cuts in. "I think maybe he's telling the truth. At least some truth."

"What?" Tinker's face is a question mark.

"I do." Mr. Madness takes three measured steps back, moving away from Agent Irving. "But I do need to make sure." Raises his gun. "Sorry, *we* need to make sure."

"You got this?" Tinker says to Mr. Madness.

"I do."

"What?" Irving's heart begins to pound. "Hold on a second."

"Hold still, Special Agent Irving." Mr. Madness takes careful aim.

"What do you want?"

"Stillness. Like I said. Please."

Hiro and Tinker smile.

Mr. Madness breathes in deeply through his nose, then fires three blasts as he exhales through his mouth.

CHAPTER 14

THE COUNTRYSIDE BLURS PAST.

The Porsche is speeding down a strap of road with nothing but open land for miles and miles around. Mother looks back through the rear window, catching a vague outline of the city behind them. She's lived in, or within a few miles of, New York City her entire life. That concrete jungle is the center of her compass and she's given little or no thought to what or who exists beyond its shadow.

Murphy grips the wheel, lost inside the deep caverns of his own mind.

A silent churning of folding ideas and crumbling memories.

"This quiet brooding bit might work with the chicks, but not with me." Mother presses a button in the door, rolling down the window. She still loves the old way of doing that.

"Little cold for windows down."

"Waking you up."

She begins playing with the air, rolling her hand and arm like waves in the breeze.

The sun warms her face as the chilly winds wraps around her, flows through her hair, and then rushes in, filling the car. Fresh, cool, clean air is something Mother didn't realize she missed while in lockup. The freedom that can come from a deep pull of air into the lungs. Little things slip from your mind as time passes inside a prison cell. Most slips are some sort of mental self-preservation, she supposes.

Murphy's eyes narrow to straining slits as he searches for something up ahead.

"Oh, I'm wide awake, Mother." His eyes widen. Found it.

Jerking the wheel hard to the right, he locks up the brakes.

Crunching gravel skids under the tires before they catch the grooves of the road, bringing the car to a jolting stop. Mother's seatbelt catches her hard across the chest and shoulder, throwing her back into the seat. She whips her head around, mouth open, milliseconds away from taking her son's head off.

Murphy gently presses her chin with his thumb, turning her head toward the right.

"There." He points to an open field next to where they are stopped.

Unbuckling his seatbelt, he slides out from the car. Mother, still pissed, follows behind him.

"Over there." Murphy shows her the patches of churned-up dirt. Motions toward the deep tracks that have been plowed up in the field. "See them?"

"Yeah. I see them. Not blind. Not yet."

"Good. That's where we died."

Mother sucks in, about to speak, but stops herself.

She looks over to him. Her son's empty expression tells her everything, no need to offer comment or ask questions. It's the drop in his eyes. How he looks lost, like he did sometimes when he was a boy. Like he did when the cops brought him home after a brutal brawl in the streets. After four kids jumped him. After Murphy put them in the hospital. This look he's holding onto right now is similar but still different. It's hard to place it.

Even for Mother.

Murphy steps toward the edge of the deepest cuts in the dirt. The land is working toward covering it all up. Nature performing its own cleanup of the evidence. But traces of the wreckage are still here. Murphy can't believe Agent Thompson and his people didn't do a better job of wiping this all away. That arrogant bastard probably didn't think he needed to.

Murphy touches the scar on his stomach.

Brubaker gave it to him.

A not-so-subtle reminder of what happened here. Brubaker used the pain of jamming a knife into his stomach to jolt his mind back to the wreck that almost cut Mr. Nice Guy Noah in half that night. His broken brain had forgotten the car crash that, for all practical purposes, ended his and his wife's lives. Hard to believe his mind would just let that slip away.

This is where it all happened.

Right here, inches from where he's standing, two lives ended, and two new ones began. He's sure their blood is mixed somewhere deep in the dirt here.

Murphy squeezes his hands tight as they start to shake.

Thoughts shift to how the steering wheel spun out from his grip. He lost control. If he had only been a little stronger that night. If he had been quicker to react. Deep inside, he knows there was nothing he could have done, even if he was Murphy that night. He also realizes both sides of his mind are trying to comfort one another. Comforting rationalizations firing back and forth like conversation between friends.

Maybe that's why he drove here.

To try and find comfort for the most uncomfortable of minds. An attempt to find a way to shut the door on all this. *To lid the thing*, as the kids say. But he feels the complete opposite. There's no feeling of closure here. Feels like that door is swinging wide open. A wide-open entrance leading into a house that's constantly on fire.

Mother keeps her distance.

Gives him space to go through whatever he's going through. She can't imagine the thoughts that are raging inside his mind. Never been a five-star parent, but her hands-off approach is actually the right call at the moment.

Murphy talks about the crash with her.

His words are soft and low.

Not the way her son normally chooses to communicate, if he chooses to speak to her at all. He tells her what happened that night. His carefully chosen words describe each moment with almost complete clarity. Every flip of the car. Every crunch of metal and bone. The searing fears. He describes how his wife was thrown out from the car. How Kate lay motionless in the field while he bled, helplessly trapped inside the twisted metal. The steel that pierced his body. Mother listens with an open heart, knowing he needs to talk it through. He has to walk it back inside his jumbled mind if he's ever going to figure out how to move forward.

A part of him wants to let it all out.

Simply wants to be heard.

He tells her what he remembers about Mr. Nice Guy Noah's final moments.

Murphy tells Mother about Mr. Nice Guy's last thoughts. About how he wished his wife Kate was still there with him. How he misses her beyond words. Beyond reason.

Mother carefully puts her arm around him and squeezes him tight. The first true moment between mother and child that she can ever remember.

What she told Peyton was true.

Murphy is different now.

But, if she's being honest, she's a little different too.

CHAPTER 15

Mr. Madness was careful when he shot Agent Irving.

All three times.

The restraint he exhibited was almost too much to bear.

He wanted to kill Irving so bad he could taste it, but Mr. Madness was intentional. Deliberate with where his bullets were placed. Took a measured, calculated risk in assuming Irving was wearing a tactical vest.

Tinker and Hiro were thinking the same thing as they did their own mental math.

Of course they did. They think the same way because Murphy thinks like this.

The tech with these tactical vests has improved greatly over the years but a single, errant, close-range blast from a 9mm can still hurt like hell. Get the wrong angle—or the right angle depending on your wants and needs—and you could still easily kill someone or put them into a vegetative state that would not be desirable.

They need Agent Irving alive, though perhaps not completely well. They need answers only he can provide.

There's a shared memory between Tinker, Hiro, and Mr. Madness. They haven't talked about it, but all three of them, at some point, have drawn on this memory in the last hour or so. It's a flash of a scene, a quick cut like it was ripped free from a movie trailer and playing at three times speed.

There's a man bleeding out in a car during intense questioning.

He's an asset. No recollection of his name or the reason for his value.

The asset's hands are soaked in his own blood, trying to stop a seeping wound in his lower abdomen. A wound that the vest should have protected him from. Mr. Madness, Tinker, and Hiro accessed this memory as if it were their own.

In a way, it is theirs now.

But it had to be Murphy's originally. No question. Nice, quiet Cody and his friends would never experience anything vaguely resembling that experience.

What normal person would?

There's a sting from another memory that's present. One of Murphy taking three shots in the chest. Spinning, turning, then tumbling off a building in Madrid. A tactical vest saved his life as he splash-landed into a body of water that they don't recall the name of.

A memory engulfed in fuzz, but it is there.

Each of these recollections are like hands grasping at drifting smoke desperate to take hold of something that can't be held. Everything in this strange highlight reel is segments of a much longer story, one they may never see or have complete access to, but the impact of the experiences is so clear at times.

Mr. Madness drew from those lessons learned as he put three bullets into the vest Irving wore. He kept them in a tight cluster—the size of a baby's fist —firing them into Irving's abdomen while standing approximately six feet away. The assumptions he made was that Irving was in decent shape, early forties, and had some level of experience in the field, considering what Irving is involved in. All that lead Mr. Madness to take the action he took. Irving also has something valuable inside his mind.

Irving said he knew where Brubaker is.

Irving said there was another member of the CIA involved. A doctor named Ernesto. And it sounded like this doctor was the one truly pulling the strings. Not poor Agent Irving. He's a messenger. A grunt. A dog. More than likely a disposable part not needed to operate the larger machinery, but he does hold information they can use. Tinker and Hiro agreed with all this as Irving lay on the barn floor twisting in pain.

Mr. Madness needs to get Brubaker free.

Tinker and Hiro want to help but value their freedom more.

They all understand that Murphy's time on this earth needs to end as well, but none of them have any desire to be attached to anyone's strings. Not Agent Irving's. Not Ernesto, and certainly not Markus Murphy. They have no interest in being a servant to anyone.

That life was for nice, quiet Cody.

The life of recovering alcoholic Tinker.

The day-to-day of Hiro as the protector of the wealthy.

This new life belongs to Mr. Madness and the two men Brubaker help set free. There's an almost constant blur overlaid across their thoughts and memories. They were all sheep, each of them in their own way, before Murphy entered their minds. That much they know with absolute certainty. They were ordinary and simple, but there was an anger beneath it all. A biting rage suppressed. Swallowed. Pushed down.

The acceptance of a wife screwing the neighbor.

The daily struggle of fighting addiction.

The absorption of the ego-fueled bullshit of big-money bosses.

They took what scraps the world left them. They snatched them up with hateful gratitude and the listless, forced smiles of an undertaker.

That was then.

This is now. And now, they have the skills to push their own agenda.

There was deep concern Mr. Madness took things too far. Maybe not as sharp with his aim as he thinks he is. He indeed has Murphy in his head, but he is still new to all this.

They all are.

Adjustment to the melding of minds can't be something that magically happens at the push of a button. The physical manifestation of all Murphy knows is still being worked out. Mr. Madness knows he might have gotten lucky with that shot he made in Central Park.

There have been headaches he has tried to ignore. Maybe nice, quiet Cody's denial of pain is coming in handy. Occasionally blood will roll out from his eyes. Most of the time it's fine, he doesn't really even notice it, but at other times the pain almost puts him down on his knees. None of the three share their experiences with one another. They don't discuss the struggles they've experienced during the transition of Murphy being jammed into their minds and lives. They suffer in silence, assuming each of them is experiencing the same level of hurt and confusion. No need to talk about it. It simply is.

In the barn, after Mr. Madness shot Irving, Hiro checked the vest to make sure a bullet didn't worm its way through to anything vital. Unlikely, but it has been known to happen. Once they realized he hadn't killed the man, Hiro removed the vest and Tinker went to work on Irving, kicking and stomping the areas he felt needed his attention.

Agent Irving's flesh was red on its way to purple.

Large, misshaped blotches of blood pooling under the skin. The bruising was severe. No doubt there was some nonlethal damage that could not be seen. The muscles will take some time to heal.

"Please take us to your friend. Dr. Ernesto, was

it?" Mr. Madness asked in a smooth and steady tone as Irving's bones crunched and cracked.

All the air was robbed from Irving's lungs as Tinker did his body work. The sound was dull and satisfying. Mr. Madness joined the work of beating their prisoner with a reserved form of glee surging through him. Irving's face was red, his eyes vacant while desperately fighting to find air as Mr. Madness and Tinker kicked him again and again.

"We're not going to kill you." Mr. Madness slicked his hair back using the sweat from his forehead. "But we will make you hurt. You know what we can do, correct?"

Irving's eyes became wide like dinner plates. His mouth opened just as wide as he finally was able to take in a breath of air. Mr. Madness and Tinker took a step back, letting him cough it out without any interference. Allowed Irving to roll around on the dirty barn floor like a wounded dog. They took a step back and took in the sight. Soaking in their ownership of him. Knowing Irving knew all about Murphy and what was streaming through their wild, unchecked minds.

That was when Agent Irving passed out.

That's also when Hiro dragged him to the car. They scooped him up, then left the barn. They needed to take this show on the road.

From the back seat of the car, Irving groans a slew of profane sentences as he tries to roll onto his side. Mr. Madness checks the rearview mirror, relived he's moving at least. He took the driver's seat even though no driver is needed.

Hiro sits in the back next to Irving while Tinker rides shotgun. Irving closes his eyes and checks out for a bit. Passing out temporarily from the pain. Thankfully there was no blood lost.

Irving groans again.

"Shit, man." He grunts.

Hiro really wishes he'd stop with the noise. There's no way they can travel with him carrying on like this.

"You awake?" Mr. Madness looks to the back seat.

"Beautiful day out," Tinker says, sipping some coffee they stopped to pick up after the barn.

"Where are you taking me?" Irving coughs hard, holding his ribs tight.

"Hoping you would tell us," Mr. Madness says. "Been waiting for some input from you."

"What do you want?"

"I think we want similar things. Maybe we do, we're not sure yet. Perhaps we don't. I don't know, but I have a feeling our wants are more similar than different."

Irving sits up, discovering his hands have been zip-tied along with his ankles.

"Is this completely necessary?"

Hiro shrugs.

"Yes, it is." Tinker glances back. "Did you somehow think we wouldn't?"

Irving looks out the window, trying to unscramble his head.

"Now." Mr. Madness holds his hands together, staring out the front windshield. "Give me a destination, then we can discuss all that remains."

"That remains?"

"Yes. What remains of your life and the value of it to us."

Irving swallows, trying hard not to show the fear that's rocketing through him. A cold line of sweat runs down the middle of his back like a car racing down the highway of his spine.

"Thought we might begin with how we get in touch with your man Ernesto." Mr. Madness raises a knife for Irving to see.

"Yeah." Tinker turns around. "That sound reasonable, Agent Irving?"

Murphy remembers.

He remembers what it was like to be two different people.

People who had separate thoughts and lives. One ended other people's lives like it was his job, and it was until recently. The other lived a modest life with his wife and two children. It's been a tug of war inside his mind ever since he woke up in that seedy motel room in New York.

He remembers the blood that dripped and spilled.

The hearts that stopped pumping because of him.

He remembers the laugh the girls have. Not the giggles, he loves those too, but the laugh of when they truly found something funny. It was deep and rich. The sound of unfiltered emotion without an agenda. Without a care or thought to anything other than the joy that comes from laughter.

He imagines the sound when they received the purple rubber ducks he sent them. They would tear open the paper with happy eyes, bouncing while holding their breath in anticipation. Waiting to release the greatest sound Murphy's mind has ever known. A precious idea Mr. Nice Guy is showing Murphy as if they were two friends sharing something wonderful.

The purity of the sound echoes through his mind.

He can't help but smile while driving the candy apple red Porsche.

"What?" Mother asks.

"Nothing."

She turns back and forth between him and the open road. They've been driving for a while. Not too long, but long enough for a moment of peace between them. Up ahead is a small town. One of many they've torn through during the great search for the best slice of pie.

"Never knew you to just randomly burst out into laughter." She scrunches her nose. "Damn creepy, man."

"Sorry."

Murphy had no idea that he was laughing. He was so lost in his own head he didn't realize he'd even made a sound. He's felt something was off the last few days. Not at first, but it has become noticeable. His denial is as strong as anyone else's, but these mental slips are becoming hard to ignore.

Am I slipping?

Are the seams of my mental stitching coming undone?

Would make sense. His mind is a mix of so many things now.

He closes his eyes, leaning his head against the window's cool glass while he loosens his grip on the steering wheel. Relaxing his thoughts, he lets the girls' laughter roll out, filling the empty corridors of this mind. A rebuilding of a space that is badly in need of repair.

He's not sorry.

Not at all.

CHAPTER 17

AGENT IRVING's trembling hand holds his ribs.

The pain is sharp.

Each breath reflects the beating he's been dealt.

With his free hand, his fingers fumble at a set of keys while trying to open a rusted gate. A pack of dogs bark their nuts off nearby. Mr. Madness follows Irving with one hand on his gun at all times. Hiro is down the street in the car just in case they need to take off in a hurry. Tinker stands at the end of the driveway. A perfect spot where Hiro can see him, and Tinker can see Mr. Madness.

Irving agreed rather quickly to take them to see Ernesto.

Mr. Madness knows there's some element of truth to what Irving has told them, but he also knows there's a far greater chance of there being lies deep within his words. More like there are large pieces of information Irving has conveniently left out.

No matter.

Mr. Madness and his friends will discover the truth. All of it. One way or another.

They pass through a yard littered with discarded bottles, fast-food wrappers, and random holes dug by some kind of animal. Feral cats scatter as they move through the center of the filth. Irving kicks a headless baby doll out of the way.

Tinker watches on, then looks back to Hiro, letting him know things are cool.

Mr. Madness thought it was foolish he was forced to more or less make one big circle to get here. Wasting time is not something he or the other two embrace. This run-down shack, this disaster of a domicile nestled amongst the trash and cats, is only a few miles from the run-down farm with the barn that posed as a safe house.

Ernesto was never far away.

But not too close either. The doctor put enough distance between himself and the safe barn to avoid getting his hands dirty or putting himself in real danger. Mr. Madness takes note of this. Tucks it away. Ernesto is the brains, and probably thinks his intelligence puts him above the nastiness of this situation he helped create. The good doctor assumes his intellectual status is understood and others will handle the unpleasant side of things. People will take care of the mess. Ernesto's arrogance has blinded him to one undeniable fact.

Mr. Madness *is* the unpleasant side of things.

Mr. Madness chose to walk with Irving to the door. He wanted to be the first inside. Wanted to be in control, set the stage for Tinker and Hiro that Mr. Madness will be running this leg of the operation until Brubaker is back.

There's a pinhole sensor light in a tree to the left of Mr. Madness, and also one to the right. Not a trip wire for something that might remove their legs. No, looks more like a security measure. An untrained eye would have missed the tiny abnormality entirely.

Thank you, Murphy mind.

Mr. Madness imagines Ernesto is seated somewhere in this run-down shack of a house watching them move through the yard. They didn't see anything when Tinker and Hiro did a sweep of the area, but they knew they would only be able to see so much. Always a possibility that Ernesto saw them coming a mile away.

Maybe he's armed himself by now.

Maybe he hasn't. Part of Mr. Madness hopes

he has as he nudges Irving with the barrel of his gun to move faster. There's an itch of anger at the back of his mind. The man behind this door did this to him. To all of them. The anger fades fast, however. Replaced by gratitude. They were all given shiny new lives because of this man.

Maybe Mr. Madness won't kill him right away.

"Just hold on, man," Irving says, sucking in a fresh batch of pain.

Mr. Madness pushes harder.

Irving takes a deep breath and knocks on the door.

A hard, single knock. Mr. Madness nods in recognition. Not something a person does. Nobody in normal society knocks on a door only once. Mr. Madness enjoys the simplicity of this final layer of security given the high-tech nature of the world today. He makes note of this as well.

Irving takes a step back, motioning for Mr. Madness to do the same.

They stare at the door for a full ten count. Then there's a series of clicks and thumps from inside the house. The thick, steel door opens. As it opens, Mr. Madness can see this is not the original door. This is a new security entrance put in to replace whatever was there before.

A small, older man steps into the doorway.

Mr. Madness has him pegged at sixty, sixty-plus years old. Thin, silver hair barely covers the top of his scalp. His back is slightly hunched over, but not too bad, with a stomach that hangs just over his belt. His black, thick glasses complete the look.

Mr. Madness does a quick scan, checking his hands and body for weapons. There's a memory of a small, frail-looking man pulling a gun on him in Chicago one sunny afternoon. The harmless-looking old man almost put a bullet in his chest that day. Murphy has some really choice experiences to mine from. It is quite something to experience. Mr. Madness fights to keep his focus on the small, older man in the doorway. He grips his gun tighter.

"Who the hell is it?" asks a woman in the background.

"Tell her to come out." Mr. Madness raises his gun, trying to see behind him.

"Okay." Ernesto raises his hands in front of his chest. Fast eyes shared between him and Irving. "It's okay."

A much younger, attractive woman appears behind Ernesto.

She's dressed in a T-shirt two sizes too small and jeans that fit like skin. Her wild eyes dance as she offers a disarming smile that's wide and warm. Her dark hair partially covers a bright-green lizard tat on her neck. The small, neon-green face peeks out when she turns her head between Mr. Madness and Ernesto. She puts one of her sculped arms around Ernesto's shoulders, giving them a hard squeeze. Mr. Madness looks to Agent Irving, looking for some form of recognition. A hint showing if he knew about this woman. The look on Irving's face bends into annoyance more than recognition.

"Having fun?" Irving asks.

Ernesto waves his hand, disregarding the question.

"Darling, please," Ernesto says to her. "May I have a moment with these gentlemen?"

"Darling?" Rolling her eyes, she slinks back into the small house.

"Where the hell did you find her?" Irving asks. "When did you have time to—"

"Stop." Mr. Madness places his gun to Irving's head. "Inside."

"Hello, Cody." Ernesto's smile is friendly, as if seeing a long-lost friend.

Mr. Madness presses his gun into Ernesto's forehead. Ernesto steps back.

"Yeah, he doesn't go by that anymore," Irving says.

"Oh?"

Mr. Madness grabs the back of Irving's neck, push-pulling him inside while steering Ernesto back with his gun. He waves his arm to Tinker, letting him know they are clear. Tinker nods, then turns to Hiro in the parked car, giving him the clear as well. Hiro starts the car. As agreed upon, he will now circle the block checking for abnormalities.

Tinker moves across the yard, cutting through the cats, taking a new position near the front door of the house. He can hear the muffled conversation inside.

Mr. Madness stands in the living room of the run-down home that looks to be doubling as a makeshift lab of sorts. Various screens line a long folding table. They flicker numbers, updating and running constant analysis. Graphs made of lines and bars light up boxes that cut up the wide-screen monitors. Several tablets with glass screens are scattered on the couch and coffee table. Stacks upon stacks of papers are piled in random locations around the room.

Mr. Madness recalls a setup similar to this.

This resembles a lab he knows.

Unlike the pang he's felt from the unfamiliar Murphy memories, this one is his. He can feel the difference. He remembers a flash of a memory. One of the lab. The one they escaped from in a whirl-wind of violence.

He was strapped down to a steel table.

Men and women in white coats were injecting things into him. His temperature was taken. His heartbeat jumped, accelerated, then evened out. The sterile room was in order. Everything in its right place save for the piles of stacked papers scattered randomly on the floor. Someone made a joke about Ernesto being *beyond old-school* with all his printed research.

"You boys knock yourself out. I'm hungry." The young woman with the lizard neck tat flips them off as she storms out the back door of the house.

Irving holds his arms out. *Really?*

"She's fine," Ernesto calms him. "She'll come back with some booze and hamburgers." He turns to Mr. Madness with a shrug. "She's a party girl. This is what she does in the afternoon."

"Does she? Is this your day now?" Irving winces as he turns faster than his ribs would like him to. "Cocktails and burgers while I'm out in the world getting the shit kicked out of me?"

Mr. Madness thinks of going after her. Something is off. He watches Tinker turn his attention to the woman as she rounds the front of the house.

"Would you like to talk about Brubaker?" Ernesto says. "That's why you're here, right?'

Mr. Madness zeros in on him. He motions to Tinker to let her go. Ernesto has had his fun with her, fulfilled his weakness, now it's time to get what Mr. Madness came for.

Tinker stands down.

"So, what should I call you now?" Ernesto asks. "If Cody is no longer correct."

"He talked about finding her." Mr. Madness pushes his chin toward Irving, who lowers himself nice and slow onto a broken-down couch. He moves a cat out of the way.

"Brubaker? That is part of the broader conversation." Ernest grins. "Yes?"

"Also said we needed to remove Murphy."

"That's also being discussed." Ernesto looks out the window. "Oh, there's Tinker. Nice guy. Is Hiro out there as well? Really nice guy—"

"Less so now." Mr. Madness lowers his gun, keeping it by his side.

Ernesto nods, understanding.

"That seems to be the case with all of you." Ernesto motions to the couch, offering him a seat next to Irving. Mr. Madness only stares back. Ernesto nods again. "It seems each day you become more and more of a rare species."

"Explain that."

"Best I can tell, there's only a handful of people who share your mindset. For lack of a better term. Now, it might be only you three, Brubaker, and yes, Markus Murphy."

"But we're not all the same."

"No, no you are not. You gentlemen and Murphy share some commonality, obviously, but there's half of you that is yours and yours alone." Ernesto offers a candy bar. Mr. Madness waves it off. "But Brubaker is different than both of you. There is no overlap in the minds. However—" Ernesto tears open the wrapper, taking a bite of the candy bar. "There's some emotional history between her and Murphy."

Mr. Madness feels his shoulders tighten. His pulse quickens as his stomach twists. A sudden, arresting feeling he was not expecting.

Mr. Madness clears his throat. "Explain that."

"Well, there's no way you would have known this, and I know all of you have an attachment to Brubaker. You were especially—"

"Stop speaking in circles, old man." Mr. Madness's face is now red. Sweat beads along his forehead.

"Brubaker was married to Murphy."

Irving shifts on the couch, as if bracing himself.

Ernesto holds Mr. Madness's stare. Locks onto the eyes of his experiment. He watches the mind of Mr. Madness flip and turn. Studies his response to the emotional swing Ernesto just took at him. Mr. Madness's eyes are hard as his body shakes. Veins plump up along his neck.

"That's not possible," he finally says. "That doesn't make—"

"You're right. As with anything in this mess, their relationship is not that simple." Ernesto again offers him a candy bar. Mr. Madness raises his gun again. Ernesto puts his hands up, backing off. "They weren't married in the classical sense. But, the other sides of them were married. The normal—again, for lack of a better term—sides of them were a couple. The nice side of Brubaker and the nice side of Murphy. They were married."

Mr. Madness wants to scream.

Wants to burn everything.

The idea that someone else was with her. That someone else knows her in that way, on that level, is too much from him to even consider. Mr. Madness has given everything to her. She is in his every thought. Contained in every breath he has. His mind shifts to his own wife. To her calling out to their neighbor while he mounted her. Her voice begging for more. He thinks of Brubaker doing the same with Murphy.

"I will kill him," Mr. Madness says.

Ernesto smiles as if he gave the correct answer to a question he hasn't asked yet.

"Good." Ernesto folds the wrapper over the uneaten half of the candy bar and places it in the refrigerator. "There's a lot to talk about, but I'd like to take a look at Irving's wounds. I'm not strictly a physician, but I was a medic in the Army years ago."

Irving pushes himself up off the couch.

Mr. Madness remembers candy bars in a bowl on a table in the lab.

"We'll get Agent Irving here put back together and get him back into the office. He needs to scour the CIA. Find out some details for us."

"Oh?" Irving moves toward them. Teeth grinding through the pain. "Do tell."

"You need to find out how to find Murphy, for one. And, check in on Brubaker." Ernesto turns to Mr. Madness. "We need to find out the best way to set her free. Right?"

Irving looks to Ernesto.

Ernesto glances his way but nothing more.

Mr. Madness nods, but can tell there's something they're not sharing with him.

Confusion is clouding everything for him. The smoky wreckage inside his mind is difficult to think through. Her relationship to Murphy is crushing every thought he has.

That was in the past, he tells himself, *and that's where we will leave it.*

His recently deceased boss used to tell him that life was through the windshield, not the rearview mirror. He hated that simplistic, bullshit expression, but in this moment, he finds odd comfort in those words. Mr. Madness knows he and Brubaker can work past this unfortunate news about her past.

He will be patient with her.

After all, she's been extremely patient with him.

Things are rarely easy between couples.

Stop!

Ernesto and Irving watch Mr. Madness rub the sweat from his forehead.

He didn't realize he said it out loud for them to hear. Or did he? Did he say anything at all, or did he actually call out like a frightened child? His mind screams out for this tumbling, spiraling thinking to end.

This is weak.

You're so fucking pathetic.

Mr. Madness looks around the room to make sure they didn't hear the pleas rambling inside his head. But looking at them, the dead silence of the room, their blank stares, he knows he allowed the inside of his mind to seep out.

He needs to stop this way of thinking.

He wants to say more. To release his searing emotions. Find a release valve to relieve the stress. Curb it, if nothing else. Must stop himself from stumbling down any long, dark hallways of thoughts. Mr. Madness bites down, digging his teeth into the flesh of his tongue. He wants the pain to stop him from thinking. To keep him from imagining a life with her. To end the longing. Snuff out the hope. To protect himself from painful ideas.

"You okay, friend?" Ernesto asks him.

Mr. Madness nods, blood tears forming, begging to fall.

"Okay." Ernesto places a hand on his shoulder with an understanding look in his eyes. "What do I call you again?"

CHAPTER 18

Irving grits his teeth as he slides down, taking a seat at his desk.

He wasn't out of the office long, but it was longer than he intended. He was also gone longer than he'd told anyone he'd be out. Of course, he can cover up the lost time with the *things happen in the field* narrative but sometimes antennas go up within the halls of the CIA when stories don't seem to line up just right.

The screen scans his face.

Studies the distance between his eyes and ears. From the tip of his nose to the corner of his right eye. Then the left. The retina scan is the final step before he's in. Allowed into the layers and layers of data the CIA captures and keeps. At least the layers to which Irving has been granted access.

Very surface and vanilla forms of data compared to some, but he's not janitorial services either. The keyboard lights up along a soft, black leather mat designed specifically for LED 3D keyboards. The synthetic leather is crafted so the keys pop visually as well as are comfortable to type upon. This process all happens in less than a blink, but Irving runs through each step in his mind every time.

He starts by searching any updates to Brubaker. Looking for notes left by other agents. Emails, digging for updates, cross-referencing others involved in projects related to her. When that bears no fruit, he moves on to finding anything about Dr. Peyton. He saves her notes for last, thinking access to those will be the most monitored. Even though he's been granted full access to her notes on Brubaker, he knows there are all kinds of eyes on what she does. And additional eyes on the eyes that watch what she does. Brubaker is the hottest topic in the CIA.

Irving stops.

He's found something.

Peyton has an unassigned block of time on a buried, limited-access team calendar. He doubts seriously she's taking a holiday. This calendar is one only he and two other people, aside from Peyton, have access to. Margo Darby is one—not a great person to ask—but the third is a newer agent who serves more as an admin than anything else.

He's a young guy.

Fresh-faced out of Camp Peary. Practically bouncing out of The Farm and eager as hell to please.

Irving springs up from his desk. Pain tears through every cell in his body. An immediate reminder of his run-in with Mr. Madness and friends. He grinds his teeth even harder as he cuts down the hall knowing the passing seconds matter. He can press the young lad without the young lad knowing he's being pressed. Time is precious right now. Irving can't allow a single word or moment go unused.

"Agent Nathan David." Irving pokes his head inside the young agent's closet of a cube. "Got a second?"

Agent David almost spills his latte down the front of his discount suit.

"Yes. Hi. How are you, Agent Irving? Good trip? When did you get back?"

"Last night. Rough flight and all that."

Agent David nods like he understands. They don't let him travel anywhere. Not yet at least.

"Hey, where's Dr. Peyton? Thought we had a meeting today."

"Oh, was I supposed to book a conference—"

"No, no, it was a quick, touching-base kind of thing. Wasn't on the books. She out of town?"

"Yeah, it was last-minute."

"Darby kind of last-minute?" Irving raises his eyebrows.

"Think so." Agent David looks both ways. "Darby was all kinds of quiet about it."

"Never a good sign."

"Not historically, no. She lit me up about a conference room one time, then got all quiet for weeks. Scared the piss out of me." Agent David catches himself. "Sorry."

"No, no, I get it. She's scary as hell." Irving remembers the dressing-down Agent David took from Darby. He sits on his desk, speaking low in a *just between you and me* tone. "Any idea where she sent Peyton in such a big-ass hurry?"

"No, but I can..." Young Agent David puts his hands down on his ancient keyboard. They won't give him a cool one. "I'm not supposed to scan the travel records. Scary Margo orders."

"Yeah. I get it, man." Irving nods, looks around. "Respect is not easily gained around here, right?"

"Absolutely." The young agent presses his lips together.

"I remember they boxed me out for years

before they let me into the party. Fought my way in is more like it. It was hard. Took some time, but I wore them down, worked my way into their good graces."

"How?"

"It's weird, man. You have to show you can do the job. Performance matters, of course, but there's also this thing where you have to show you're one of them. You know? Team guy and all that. I have some college buddies who work in tech and it's the same shit there too; you have to get the *high-ups* to like you. Somehow."

The young agent shakes his head.

"I know." Irving rolls his eyes. "I know it's junior high type bullshit but it's real, man. People, no matter the profession, like to work with people they like. Or, at the very least, people they can tolerate."

Irving pretends to think about it, then checks both ways.

"Look, man. There's a happy hour some of us go to. Nothing crazy, just a dive bar for a few drinks. My level. A few show up that are higher." Irving is almost in his ear. "Maybe you pop in one night. Have a beer or two. Smile. Laugh at their jokes. Tell some young guy stories. Nothing these dinosaur douchebags like more than that."

Agent David's eyes light up.

"You think so?"

"Fucking know so."

Placing his fingers back on the keyboard, Agent David's mind rips through the possibilities.

"Now." Irving leans over his shoulder. "I only need to know where she landed, and maybe just in general, why she went there. I can take it the rest of the way." Irving holds out his arms. "Help me out, brutha?"

CHAPTER 19

THIS IS IT.

The grandaddy of them all.

Number one on the list.

The best slice of pie in the country.

Some would argue on the planet. This time, these words are not just some biased, homespun hyperbole. Not some braggadocio small-town marketing blah-blah. What lies beyond the glass doors of this establishment has been voted upon. Vetted. Due diligence performed. Heated competitions awarded by an impressive panel of expert judges.

The slice of apple voted number one is here.

Along with the number one cherry and the number two blueberry.

The first one, the apple, was unanimous. No

argument spoken nor could one be made. But the cherry was somewhat controversial. The blueberry fell anywhere from one to four on most ballots, with the average landing it in the two slot by mere basis points. But make no mistake, there's some damn fine pie eating beyond these doors.

Murphy's fingers tingle with excitement.

Mother can't stand it. She wants to throw open the doors and run in like a child screaming with arms flailing.

This is their moment. A moment they've earned, dammit.

Pushing open the doors, they both fight to hold it together. In a calm and orderly fashion, they enter and, in a pleasant tone, kindly ask the hostess for a table for two. Pete's Perfect Pies is not a huge place, but it is bigger than any of the other spots they've been to. Probably needed the extra space to handle all the foot traffic their accomplishments have generated for them over the years.

The waitress stands by their table.

Her smile is wide, warm, nice as can be.

They both order coffee, then decide to start off by sharing a slice of the blueberry. An appetizer of sorts. Wet the beak, if you will. They will cleanse the palate with a second cup of coffee, then share a slice of the cherry. Then, of course, that world-beater of a pie—a thick-cut slice of apple. There is no rush. No need to shove this experience along in a hasty fashion. This may very well be the top of the mountain for these two.

This is what they've been searching for ever since Murphy picked Mother up from prison in that classic red Porsche 911. Never in a billion years would either of them imagine this is where they would be, given their history. If you'd told them a few weeks ago how things would work out, they'd have called you a few choice, horrible names, then perhaps punched you in the face.

This is a new world for them both.

One they should have been a part of years ago but had no idea how to get there. It's been a strange trip for Murphy. A lot of pain received and given to get to this spot. His mind is still, at best, a twirling mess of bloody conflicts and mushroom clouds of confusion. The starts and screeching halts of thoughts and memories are a constant struggle to reconcile. He's worked to try and not categorize them. Tried to not label them Murphy's or Mr. Nice Guy's. Some are obvious, not much he can do about those. Murder and mayhem belong in one basket, but he wants to accept the collective experience as theirs. No need to assign names to them. It's exhausting. Not productive, either.

He looks to Mother as she stirs her coffee.

Her eyes light up as the thick slice of warm blueberry pie is placed in the center of the table. Two forks. One plate. She waits for Murphy to take the first fork. He politely declines, giving her the honors.

Murphy remembers when he was much younger. The way Mother stood in the corner while he fought one of her boyfriends. During his early years, he lost those fights. He'd learn. Absorb the pain. Swallow the rage. Later, as time went on, he won more and more of them. Put a few of her "special friends" into the hospital. She watched on while these fights got meaner. Tougher. More violent. She'd stare at him with apologetic eyes but never offered an apology.

He knows he'll never get one.

Murphy watches her enjoy the pie. Not long ago, these memories would have put him into an instant state of anger. His rage would have been immediate and possibly uncontrollable. He'd want to scream at her. Put a fist through a wall. But now he doesn't feel the need for any of that.

He's different.

In ways too numerous to count. Accepting the past for what it was is an option for him now that wasn't there before Dr. Peyton and friends changed him forever.

Murphy takes a forkful of pie.

The crust is flakey with the oh so satisfying feeling of a soft crunch as his teeth sink in. The blueberries are not overpowering but you know they are there. Mother's eyes almost roll back into her skull. Murphy nods. No words needed. Their forks clink as they battle for another bite.

This is the life Dr. Peyton envisioned for her patients.

Murphy sees that now. He didn't get it completely when she passionately explained it to him at that hotel in New York. Everything was too fresh. No way to grasp all the details. But what Murphy is experiencing at this very moment is what Peyton wanted. He hopes she works out the bugs, because if every subject has to go through what Murphy went through, this ain't gonna work.

Murphy snickers at the thought.

"What's up with you?" Mother asks.

"Nothing."

"Just a little giggle box today?"

"That's right."

"Bullshit."

Murphy licks his fork clean. "You don't need to know everything."

"Fair." She looks around the packed restaurant. "Where's that damn slab of cherry?"

"And the best apple pie in the history of apples."

"Correct." Mother stabs her demanding finger on the table. "Get that bitch Pete in here and find out where in the sweet hell is our sweet-ass apple pie."

They share a laugh. They could barely carry on a conversation over the phone a few days ago. He was in a Bagdad resort. She was in prison. Today they are sharing laughs at Pete's Perfect Pies.

Life does move pretty fast.

"Sorry," Dr. Peyton interrupts. "Please don't kill me."

Murphy and Mother drop their forks.

"I mean seriously, please don't kill me," Peyton stresses.

"What do you want?" Mother picks up her fork.

"You know they aren't going to give up," Peyton says. "The CIA isn't simply going to let this go."

"They can eat dick," Murphy says.

"Be that as it may—"

"You still following us?" Murphy forks some pie, offering Peyton some.

"No." Peyton waves off the pie.

"She hasn't been following us?" Murphy asks Mother.

"Seems like she's following us," Mother says.

"I've been followed before and this seems a lot like she's—"

"No. Yes." Peyton takes a seat. "Yes, I have been following you. Never stopped, you know that. And no, I don't want any of that goddamn pie."

"Rude as hell." Mother tries to flag down a waiter. "I'll get you a plate."

"I don't want—"

"You need a plate," Murphy says. "You like following us around, Dr. Stalker?"

"You enjoy following those children?" Peyton stares at Murphy.

His face drops.

"That was not part of the deal. A deal that you agreed to."

"Not sure my attorney"—Murphy motions to his mother—"ever saw a formal, executed contract."

Mother shakes her head with her cheeks bulging with pie.

"They'll know if you get within a hundred yards of those kids, Murphy. Agents will swarm if you get within fifty. You were lucky this time. You got way too close to that family, but I was monitoring you closely that day so I called off the dogs. They wanted to send a team in."

It's as if all the air was sucked out of the room.

Murphy had always suspected they were watching him, but he didn't know to what extent. The word Peyton used—*family*—stabs at him like an ice pick. Those are his children. His girls.

We gave them up, man.

So they could have a better life. They can still have a great one. We've been over and over this.

Made the best of a shitty hand.

"You were specifically told to stay away. You asked to stay away. If for no other reason, it was for their protection. We can't have you..." Peyton feels all the guilt for what she's saying. For what she's about to tell him. "They're being moved."

"What?" Murphy's expression drops.

"We're moving them to a neighborhood you don't know." She holds up a hand, attempting to reassure him. "Somewhere nice. Safe. Great schools. But a location you will not know."

Murphy fingers dig into the table. The idea of the girls being moved somewhere unknown plunges deep like blade made of ice pushing slowly between his ribs.

"You here to shame me into working with those assholes? That the thing?"

"If that's what it takes, sure. Not above it."

Mother's frustration grows as she tries and fails to get a waiter to come over to the table.

"I have zero interest in working for the CIA or anyone else. Also part of my deal."

"While that might have been implied in your mind, it wasn't necessarily part of the agreement."

Her words—*in your mind*—dig into the meat of his thoughts as if her words had claws. His mind is at the center of all this. The seed of all that's happened. The reason for this conversation.

Mother finally gets the attention of a man.

Not dressed as a waiter but has a certain service look to him. He's very dialed in on their table. *Maybe he's management*, she thinks. Seems a little ragged, a little creepy, but he's paying attention to them at least. He smiles as he moves toward the table.

Perhaps that's Pete, she thinks.

"I'm a free man." Murphy pinches some flakey crust, tossing it in his mouth.

"You're a science experiment that is still evolving."

"That's sweet. So glad you stopped by."

"Murphy, I'm sorry. I'm not here to fight or to make things worse than they are, but there are some realities that we have to face." Peyton resets. "We've seen shifts in the other subjects like you."

"Shifts? Subjects?"

"Almost like parts of their personalities are collapsing."

"I'm strong like bull."

Mother laughs, almost choking on her pie. She continues to wave the manager over to the table.

"I have something I need to give to you," Peyton continues. "A quick injection. Not a long-term solution by any stretch of the imagination, but we've run some tests and what I have is a tempo-rary fix."

"Peyton, greatly appreciated but—"

"It's an advanced SSRI."

Murphy blinks.

"Selective Serotonin Reuptake Inhibitor." She reaches for her bag. "Modified to fit within your special circumstance—"

Murphy places a hand on her elbow. Not incredibly forceful but enough to get her attention.

"I'm fine." Murphy stops, realizing. "Wait. Is this about her? Is Brubaker okay?"

"Murphy." Peyton pauses, considers. "There is something else."

"Spill it, doc."

Her lips part, about to answer.

The manager clears his throat, now standing at the front of the table.

His hair is ratty. His clothing is hipster disheveled.

"Yes?" Mr. Madness asks. "How can I help?"

"Pie. The apple pie. Our apple pie." Mother's blood simmers. "Where in the hell is my pie?"

Mr. Madness turns his attention to Murphy.

Murphy can't place him, but there's something with this guy. Something about him that rings a bell to Murphy. Can't specifically remember how he knows him, but there is a look and feel to him that drips with a thick goo of familiarity.

"Have we met?" Murphy asks.

"Possible." Mr. Madness adjusts his shirt, breaking eye contact. "Another life, perhaps?"

Murphy catches a quick glance of the outline of a gun under his shirt. Tucked into the front of his jeans. Murphy's fingers begin to tingle. He slows his breathing, steadies his pulse. Keeping a calm mind and an active body is what someone once told him was the key. The key to killing without getting killed.

"Okay. Another life, you say?" Murphy clucks his tongue. "That's kinda fun. Dated, labored and tired, but an almost fun response. Now seriously, man. Where do I know you from?"

Peyton turns toward Murphy. Her heartrate ticks up as she catches the look on his face. She's witnessed this vibe before. Never a good sign.

"No. Can't say I've had the pleasure, sir." Mr. Madness is ice. His words flat.

Mother doesn't like it. She grips her fork, moving it under the table.

"You sure about that, friend?" Murphy asks.

It's his eyes. More like what's floating behind them that Murphy is dialing in to.

"We are not friends," Mr. Madness corrects him.

Last time Murphy felt this odd, unexplainable connection was in Montauk. That night he got into a nasty gunfight with multiple people who shared his mind. Brubaker's people. It was all in their eyes too. Also, in the way they spoke. Not unlike the way this guy is speaking. It's a feeling that can't be easily defined but it cannot be mistaken for anything else. Murphy's hand moves toward his Glock that he has tucked behind his back.

He can put two in this man's sternum, then one between his eyes.

"I know you would like to put two in my sternum," Mr. Madness says. "Then one between my eyes."

Murphy's blood runs cold.

"I know this, because you know this."

"Central Park." Murphy snaps his fingers as his memory clicks into place. "You're the asshole who made that sick headshot at the bridge."

Mr. Madness nods.

"Not too many folks could make that shot."

"Correct. I doubt few could."

"I can make that shot."

"I know you can." Mr. Madness presses his palms down flat on the table. "I suggest we place our hands in a peaceful, resting position. Let's attempt to communicate without looming threats."

Mr. Madness turns, spotting a man standing near the restrooms. Peyton sees him too.

"Murphy—" Peyton starts.

"Tell me you have something helpful to add," Murphy says.

"That guy over there." Peyton zeros in on the man. "His name is Tinker."

"This is correct," Mr. Madness adds.

"He escaped from the lab with Brubaker." She

knows the faces from the security footage better than she knows the faces of her own family. Holding her breath, she spots another familiar face. "And that guy by the door. His name is Hiro."

A large Japanese man has taken a position near the front entrance.

Peyton turns back to Mr. Madness. "You I don't recognize."

"He's wearing a shit wig," Murphy cuts in. "So, you've got an armed goon at the entrance and another near the kitchen. Smart. Nice little box you've put us in."

Mr. Madness nods.

Murphy glances to Mother ever so slightly, then removes his hand from his Glock, placing both hands flat on the table and spreading his fingers wide.

He raises his eyes to meet Mr. Madness. *Now what?*

"Good." Mr. Madness swallows hard. Blinks away an odd flash of emotion. "I'd like to talk about—"

"You okay there?"

"Yes, of course. I'm fine." Mr. Madness fights to pull it together. "I'd like to talk about your wife."

Murphy's eyes narrow, taking in the sudden redness rushing into Mr. Madness's cheeks. The tight tension in his shoulders. There's been a massive shift in the mood and body language of this man who was so calm and cool only seconds ago.

"Who?"

"Brubaker. Lady Brubaker I believe you called her."

"She's not my wife."

"In a way she is."

"In a big way she's not."

Mr. Madness begins to shake.

"Part of her, part of you were together." He barely gets it out. "She's not for you anymore."

Murphy stares back, offering him nothing. This guy is on the edge. Murphy needs to push him off. He makes quick eyes to Mother again. She's on the same page.

"Do you understand what I'm saying to you?" Mr. Madness presses his hands harder on the table. His face races through shades of red. Spit drips from his lower lip. "Tell me you understand. You of all people should understand, about her. She needs to be rid of everything about you."

"Tell you what, bro." Murphy musters the most condescending tone he can produce. "I understand that you sound slightly smitten."

"And gross," Mother adds.

"Creepy too," Murphy says.

Mother and Peyton both nod.

"Don't do that." Mr. Madness slams his hands down on the table. Plates and glasses bounce. "Do not do that."

The other diners begin to take notice, looking over at their table. Murphy catches a glance at a woman sitting alone at a table next to them. She turns away, showing off a neon-green lizard tattoo on her neck. Odd for a place like this, but not completely off.

"Don't do what?' Murphy asks, turning back. "What am I doing?"

"I know." Mr. Madness is locked in on Murphy. Furious eyes boring through him. "You are fully aware—"

"No. What exactly am I doing?"

"You're trying to upset me."

"Am I?" Murphy smiles. "Am I upsetting you, friend?"

"Stop calling me your friend. I am not your—"

"Then what should I call you?" Murphy looks again to Mother.

She gives an ever-so-slight nod.

Dr. Peyton widens her feet under the table, pressing them hard to the floor, knowing she will need a solid stance in order to move fast. No matter what happens. Not her first rodeo.

"They call me Mr. Madness."

"Holy shit. Really?" Murphy bites his lip, fighting back a laugh. "Wow."

Mr. Madness balls up his fists. Veins pop.

"Who's ready for the world's best apple pie?" A cheery, rail-thin waiter has moved next to the table.

"Now," Murphy says to Mother.

Mother stabs Mr. Madness in the hand with her fork. Jamming it with all she has into the table before shoving herself back stumbling out from her chair.

Peyton grabs her fork. The waiter drops the pies. The plates crash to the floor and shatter into a collection of chunks and tiny pieces.

Murphy fires straight up, pulling his Glock and placing it an inch from Mr. Madness's right eye. The customers nearby start running for the exits. Bolting toward safety. Screams fill the air. Tables and chairs are tossed aside or sent tumbling, bouncing off the tile. The shock on everyone's faces punches pinholes in Murphy.

Not sure he's seen this response to violence in a long time. The distance in their expressions. As if their world has been invaded by a form of ugliness they've only seen on small screens held in their hands.

Peyton keeps her attention on Tinker and Hiro.

They hold strong at their positions, only now they stand with weapons pulled.

The waiter stands planted to the floor.

"Run," Murphy tells him.

The waiter takes off, stumbling over a knocked-down table next to him. Mr. Madness grinds his teeth, wiggling the fork back and forth, trying to work it free from his hand. Blood seeps out around the sides of the four holes.

"Leave it, asshole." Murphy presses the gun into his eye socket. "Okay, Mr. Madness. How did you find me? Who are you with?"

Mr. Madness's entire body shakes. Sweat drips.

From the edge of his periphery, Murphy sees Tinker drifting nice and slow toward them.

"Fine." Murphy whips his gun to the left.

He fires two blasts, each shot tagging Tinker in the chest, sending him spinning backward down to the floor.

Hiro moves toward them. Charging hard.

"That's two in his sternum. Guessing he's wearing a vest. Truly hope not, but that's what I'd have on, and since we're all of like mind around here..." Murphy returns his gun to Mr. Madness's head. "I do still need to put one in someone's head. Got this compulsion for completion, ya know?"

Mr. Madness holds up a hand telling Hiro to stand down.

Hiro slows to a stop in the middle of the now almost-empty diner. The last echo of the crowd's panic drifts into the sounds of classic pop music playing from above.

"Good boy," Murphy tells Hiro. "Please plant your big ass right there."

Murphy watches as dark-red trails stream down Mr. Madness's face. Blood tears falling down from the eyes. Murphy forgot about the tears of blood that fell from his own eyes not long ago.

He remembers all too well the fear that goes with them.

That arresting feeling is still fresh in his mind. In a flash, the momentum of the moment slams into him like a runaway train. This man, this Mr. Madness, is experiencing the same thing that Murphy has. He shakes his head, attempting to free his mind of this.

Not now, Mr. Nice Guy.

Empathy is not the word of the day.

Let me take the wheel, buddy.

The hand holding his Glock starts to tremble. His vision tilts. Stepping back ever so slightly, his gun pulls away. Mr. Madness yanks the fork from his hand.

"Murphy!" Mother screams.

Murphy's eyes are vacant. Lost.

Dr. Peyton makes a move for her bag that still sits by her chair.

Mr. Madness pulls his gun. Murphy steps further back, almost falling over his own feet. Peyton fumbles around inside her bag, pulling a syringe out. Mr. Madness levels his gun on Murphy.

Mother picks up her chair and swings it like a war hammer. The chair cracks Mr. Madness in the back and jolts him from the aim he had on Murphy.

A single bullet fires from his gun.

Peyton spins as the bullet carves into her flesh. A pop of blood and bone between her neck and shoulder. The syringe drops to the floor.

Hiro storms over with his gun blazing.

Bullets whiz past Murphy, who stands motionless amongst the chaos.

As if he's watching a video in slow motion. A spectator in a world he's not a part of. He sees the rage in Hiro. The fire of his gun exploding in his direction but missing to the left. Part of Murphy thinks Hiro must be still be adjusting to the gun. His two minds must not have synced up completely. The knowledge of the weapon is there but the physical use of it is still a work in progress. Otherwise Murphy would be dead.

Wake up! His insides claw and scream.

Mr. Madness adjusts, turns his gun back on Murphy. Murphy looks to him, knowing this guy's marksmanship is fully online. Mother launches herself across the table, sending the plates and glasses flying in every direction.

Snap out of it or you're all dead.

Mr. Madness fires, this time at Mother. A hole explodes in the wood, almost splitting the table in two. Mother lands on the other side, taking the gun from Murphy's hand. She spins around and squeezes off two shots that fire wild.

Bullets zip by Mr. Madness's ear.

Hiro wraps his hands around Murphy's throat. His thick hands squeeze hard, shutting down the flow of oxygen to almost nothing.

Sirens wail outside. Hints of red and blue lights flash through the windows.

Mr. Madness kicks what's left of the table over onto Mother as she fires again. Mr. Madness runs toward the kitchen, pushing through what's left of the staff seeking refuge. He shoves, stepping over or on those who remain in the diner.

"Move," Mr. Madness calls out to Hiro.

Hiro and Murphy lock eyes.

Murphy shakes. His mind spinning and helpless. Like watching everything from inside of a dead body. Unable to engage. Locked, trapped inside a coffin of meat and bone that will not respond no matter how much he'd like it to.

Mother puts the gun to Hiro's head.

Hiro slaps her, sending her flying into a pile of chairs.

Murphy's world floods back online as he watches Mother fall. A string has been pulled. He unleashes a blitz of punches on Hiro. Thumps of fists on meat. Hiro steps back, absorbing the blows, and raises his gun, squeezing off multiple shots.

Murphy hits the floor and rolls for cover.

Hiro moves fast, moving toward Tinker. He tries to pick up his friend, to carry him over his shoulders wounded-soldier style. Mother scrambles on the floor away from the chairs, firing twice. Tinker slips from Hiro's grasp, sliding back to the floor as the bullets scream overhead. Mr. Madness yells for Hiro from the kitchen as the sound of the sirens gets closer and closer.

Mother fires again.

Hiro's skin rips as a bullet grazes his thick shoulder. Mr. Madness grabs him by the arm, dragging him away from Tinker toward the kitchen.

Once they're gone, Mother crabwalks across

the floor to her son. She holds Murphy's face in her hands, looking into his eyes. Inspecting, looking for answers.

She slaps the hell out of him.

Murphy shakes his face hard.

She slaps him again, only harder.

He grabs her hands, then nods.

Got it. Enough.

Mother stares, letting him know this will be discussed later. Moving quick, Mother checks on Dr. Peyton. Peyton holds her wound while lying on the diner's tile floor. Blood creeps between her fingers.

"Give that to him." Peyton coughs out the words while motioning to the syringe a few inches from her stretching fingers. "We think it'll lower the potential for crashing."

"Potential for crashing?" Mother asks. "My boy just crashed."

Murphy moves over next to them as the police swarm the diner outside.

"I'm fine," he says, attempting to defuse the concern.

Tires screech. Car doors slam shut. Voices bark orders. They'll be inside any second now. Mother decides now is not the time to get into her son's state of mind.

"The balance is tricky with you." Peyton smiles to Murphy. She's fading fast. "Damn split-heads. Killing me."

Murphy watches her eyes close as her body shuts down reacting to the shock and pain.

A single tear of blood rolls down his face.

CHAPTER 21

FIRST RESPONDERS HAVE BLANKETED the diner.

Police and EMS weave in and out, assessing the damage.

The once comfortable, casual safe haven where families and friends came together to enjoy a famous slice of pie has now become a crime scene. The unthinkable has landed at the front door of their tiny community. They'd all heard about the riots in the city. Considered those big-city problems that didn't affect their angelic lifestyle. There's a dull murmur of emergency personnel as they work their impossible task of restoring calm. Still, through it all, the smell of freshly baked pie radiates in the air.

Cops close in on Murphy and Mother with guns drawn.

Mother puts her hands up high above her head. Murphy blinks. His expression blank. Eyes are dark, empty holes where windows for emotions should be.

The cops bark orders at him.

Murphy stares into tiny pinpricks of red light on their vests. Their body cams are filming all this. Murphy knows the images they are capturing of him will be taken, seized by the agency or erased completely. Oh yes, the CIA will swoop in soon. They know Peyton is here. They'll want to know everything Murphy and Mother have to offer. Which isn't a lot.

Murphy slumps down to the floor.

Thoughts blur then break, crumbling apart, floating into fragments of memories and ideas. The pieces of Murphy and Mr. Nice Guy are a jumbled mishmash of experiences the two have lived. Some happy. Most not. Some shared. Most not. Both working to parse what has happened.

Murphy feels people surrounding him.

Can hear the voices. He can hear Mother too.

Murphy remembers everything from Lady Brubaker. Those memories are clear as they can be. They are fresh and new. Ones both Murphy and Mr. Nice Guy had together. These are rare. Memories from the moment Peyton told him about the mixing of minds will be theirs. Murphy and Mr. Nice Guy's. Not thoughts that have the pang of separation. He knows those will have the most weight going forward. The experiences they've had together.

He remembers meeting Brubaker at the resort bar in Iraq. The room where she stabbed him. She spoke in sentences of sharp, broken glass. The crazed, manic look she had in that street in New York when he aided in her capture. Mr. Nice Guy steps into the memory mix with something about his family. As if he tossed in an opinion from the back of the class. It's a flash of something wonderful. A thought about his girls. The girls, and the life he shared with the kind half of Brubaker. The life he had with his wife, Kate.

Murphy feels hands on him.

He's being lifted, moved. A rush of wind whips around him. He's being moved outside. The world outside his mind is a smeared version of reality. A car door shuts. He's lying down. His fingers can feel cool leather beneath him. An engine starts. There are sounds and colors, but they cannot be molded into anything understandable.

Nothing clear.

Nothing to hold on to.

Murphy's thoughts wander back to the girls.

He wants to slap himself. Force himself to snap out of it. He's been through this. They've moved past all this shit. Murphy and Mr. Nice Guy Noah have an agreement. They agreed the past is done. They are moving on with what they have. Playing the hand they've been dealt.

Period.

He screams and claws at the walls of his busted brain, knowing that it's a wasted effort. None of this is easy. None of this is going to be that simple. He's slipping, dropping down into a deeper place inside his mind. He's been here before. This sensation of sliding into a tub of warm milk is familiar. His mind is shutting down. To call it sleep would be an insult.

This is something else.

An electric current of anxiety splinters through his head.

His body jolts. Not awake but not asleep either. Murphy checked out but has no idea for how long. Still lying down, but he knows he's somewhere else. Feels different. The air has a new feel to it. Cool yet sticky. He's been sweating. The sounds of muffled chaos have stopped. Through the fog of his partial vision, Murphy locks in on something beyond the blur.

A small object is moving toward him.

He's changing. He knows it. Feels like honey sinking into the nooks and crannies of warm toast. Something is happening to him on a chemical level. It's been coming on for days. Peyton said she thought they were crashing. Did she mean they were falling apart? Peyton told him once that everything was rushed. Proper monitoring and testing were pushed aside. They didn't completely know the effects or what would happen. Only educated guesses and theories. Is the science that brought Murphy's mind together failing? Is that what's been happening?

The boxing ring. The firing range.

The headaches. The dreams.

Is Murphy coming undone?

The small object seems as if it is levitating toward him. Metallic. Made of steel, perhaps. Light bounces off the longer edge of it. Fingers hold it steady. He tries to fight what is coming toward him. He thrashes best he can, but forceful hands hold him down.

Mr. Nice Guy tries to soothe him. Comforting phrases a parent would tell an anxious child. Well-meaning lies saying that everything will be okay. There's nothing to worry about. Some bullshit about it always being darkest before the dawn.

Even Mr. Nice Guy doesn't believe the shit he's slinging.

He's shaking. Teeth begin to chatter. His temperature is dropping.

He was fine. His mind was finding solid ground.

It was going to be okay. Things were going to work out.

Things are not okay.

Nothing is ever going to be okay.

"Murphy." Mother gives his face a soft slap. "Here."

A bright light goes supernova, washing away his view. Some incoherent growls from a familiar source. Murphy's eyes snap into focus. As the fog drifts, peeling away from his vision, he realizes the small, levitating metal object is a fork. A fork that carries what he assumes is a hearty bite of the world's best apple pie. Mother sits on the floor next to him in a small, nondescript room. A take-out container of half-eaten pie sits open next to her.

Wait.

Did she already eat half of it? Did she take a snack break?

Murphy thinks about addressing the issue but accepts the bite of pie instead. It's still warm. The crust melts in his mouth. The apples are soft, but a bit of a crunch remains. He swallows it down as the taste of lingering heaven coats his tongue. Feels the start of a smile. He yanks it back as if joy is kept on a tight leash. Something normal is still in here. Something as simple as a pie is grounding him and his wildfire mind. He's encouraged, feels at least a little more tethered to the here and now.

He opens his eyes.

"Crazy shit-fuck tasty," Mother says. "Right?"

Murphy can't argue. He looks around. The room is bare. Nothing but crushing beige-colored walls. No windows, with only a single steel door that leads to somewhere unknown. His head floods with thoughts of the diner.

"Did everybody get out of the diner?"

"Look at you." She smiles. "Concerned for others and shit."

Murphy wants to punch her.

"They're lucky as hell," Mother says. "They don't know it, but they are. That whole thing could have easily gone the way of a full-blown massacre."

Murphy's head turns, eyes dart, searching for Peyton.

"She's over there." Mother points with her fork.

Behind Murphy, Dr. Peyton is laid out on a small inflatable mattress. She looks to be uncon-scious but has received some medical attention.

Fresh bandages for her wound. There's a glass of water with a straw by the bed along with an IV hanging from a stand set at half its maximum height. Murphy can see her blanket rise and fall. The sight of her breathing makes him breathe easier.

"She going to be okay?" he asks.

"They didn't really say."

"Who?"

Mother jams a needle into his neck.

"What the hell?"

"Sorry." Said with zero apology to her voice.

Warmth flushes through his neck, spreading fast throughout his body. His sight goes white for a fraction of a second, then melts into a jigsaw version of the world. Like looking through a sliced-up waterfall. A metallic taste overpowers the wonderful aftertaste of pie. His eyes fill, he blinks away the tears. Mother wipes under his eyes, scrunching her nose while inspecting the red-stained napkin.

"You're a damn mess, kid," she says.

"I know."

"What are we going to do with you?"

"Shoot me?"

"Maybe." Mother loads up some more pie. "But not today."

Murphy opens up like a baby bird so Mother can feed him some pie.

"Markus Murphy?" a woman's voice asks.

Murphy and Mother turn, looking up toward a woman who's standing over them. The woman is surrounded by tall men in gray suits with perfect hair and serious looks. The woman wears a maroon suit with her shoulder holster in clear view. Mother pulls her hand back, leaving the fork hanging from Murphy's lips.

"How is the apple?" Agent Margo Darby gives a thin smile. "Heard it's to die for."

"HI, MY NAME IS MARKUS MURPHY." An insane smile spreads. "What the hell do you want?"

Agent Margo Darby studies him.

"Okay." Tries another question, pointing back toward Peyton. "Is she going to be okay?"

Darby continues looking him over in silence, as if he hasn't said a thing. Murphy thinks of when Mother did the same thing to him. People want to see if they can get a look at the second person inside of him. It's annoying as hell, but Murphy gets it to a certain extent. He tried to do the same with that wackadoo Mr. Madness. He lets her stare for a few beats, until he can't take it anymore.

"You done?" he asks. "Think you can answer me now?"

"Apologies." Darby shrugs. "You do understand how fascinating you are, right?"

"He's a wonder, all right," Mother chimes in.

"You know..." Darby turns to her, but her eyes look toward the men in gray suits she walked in with. "I think you should get checked out. I saw you take that nasty dive across that table."

"Don't. Don't shepherd me off to some bullshit—"

"I'm only suggesting that you might have some injuries that are currently being masked by adrenaline and/or a deep, understandable concern for your son."

"Oh, you can suck a—"

"Mother," Murphy cuts in. He'd like to talk with this Agent Darby that Peyton has told him so much about. Like to chat to her without Mother's *help*. "She's right. You should get looked at."

"What?" Mother's face is turning redder by the second.

"Just to be on the safe side."

"Safe side?" Mother laughs. "Like that's a thing you know anything about."

"Mother, please." Murphy tilts his head toward Darby.

Mother gets it. Her son wants to work her alone. She doesn't like it, but she moves along with the men in the gray suits who tower over her like trees. She made sure to pick up the container of pie before she got up. Murphy shakes his head.

"Don't touch me," she says as she's escorted away.

The agents exit with Mother through the steel door. As they do, through the doorway Murphy sees what looks like a pretty nice house. Seems to be well-furnished with some style and a curated, decorator's touch. He even caught a whiff of something cooking, along with the sound of a television playing.

"What the hell? I'm going out there." He waves his arms around. "This room is shit."

Darby motions for an agent standing near the door, asking the last remaining man in gray to get them some coffee and a couple glasses of water. The man obeys without a hint of question or attitude. The way these guys respond to her isn't lost on Murphy.

This Agent Darby is without question the person running the show.

She's the one running Peyton, which in turn, means she's trying to run him. He's making an assumption, but even in today's so-called modern world an African-American woman in the CIA has had to bury more than a few bodies to get where she is. Literally and figuratively. Murphy feels he can safely assume Margo Darby will go from peaceful to nuclear in a snap.

"To answer your second question—and I will get to the first one, the one about what the hell I want—I don't know about Dr. Peyton's wounds. She's resting now, and my guess is she'll be okay. We have some expert medical professionals in another room."

Agent Darby lowers, sitting with her legs crossed on the floor next to him. She did it in a single, smooth motion, gliding down to the floor without a hint of awkwardness or strain. Murphy takes note that this woman is strong inside and out. Yoga, maybe. Perhaps a Western and/or Eastern martial arts discipline she picked up. She moves like a boxer, but there're other influences there to be sure.

"And I assure you"—she holds up a hand—"we have extra security protocols here at the house."

Murphy detects a slight hint of a Southern accent when she speaks. It comes and goes with certain words. Nothing crazy, but it's there.

"Why on earth would we need extra security, Agent Margo Darby?"

"Darby is fine." Darby rubs her chin.

"Darby it is."

"We believe Dr. Peyton might be a target."

"Do you?"

"Believe you are as well."

"Been a target for quite some time."

"True, but not like this." Margo Darby thumbs toward the other side of the room. "I like Dr. Peyton, I really do, and we will do everything to help her. But, if I'm being honest, this does give me an amazing opportunity to talk with you. One you and I might not have otherwise."

One of the agents in gray enters holding two cups of steaming coffee, another close behind holding two glasses of ice water, and a third with cream and sugar. Darby mouths a *thank you*, then waves off the men in gray as she turns back to Murphy. She waits for the door to shut, then pauses as the faint hum of white noise is pumped into the room.

Murphy nods, acknowledging that this is no ordinary house. This is one set up specifically for the CIA's wants and needs. Darby nods back, picks up her coffee, then starts in with her conversation.

"Want to tell me what happened with you today?"

"What do you mean?"

"I saw the security footage from the pie place. Not sure I love the idea of living in a world where

Pete's Perfect Pies needs six eyes in the sky to feel safe, but that's neither here nor there. What's more important is what I saw. And what I saw was that you froze up when you could have taken those guys out."

"Interesting interpretation."

"Your mother saved your ass."

Murphy bites back a response. Fairly obvious Darby made that remark to get a heated retort. He did the same with Mr. Madness. Murphy has no desire to let Darby have what she wants.

"Maybe I didn't feel like hurting anyone."

"Sure." Darby holds back a laugh. "From what I've seen, that would be a first for you." Darby resets. "That needle your mother jammed in your neck, the one Peyton tried to hand you at the diner, you feeling any better?"

"Better is a loose term, but I'm trending toward normal."

"Whatever *normal* means, right?"

Murphy doesn't bother responding.

"You've got questions for me. As I have for you, but I can wait." Darby takes a sip of coffee, making a *that's good* face. "So please, fire away. Might not have all the answers, but I'll tell you what I can."

"Doesn't really matter, does it? You're only going to tell me what you want me to hear."

"So you're familiar with how we work."

"Painfully."

"Look, man." Darby leans in with her best *I'm going to level with you* expression. Murphy's seen this with agents in the big bad CIA. She'll toss in some profanity soon to show that she's opening up. "We're the fucking CIA. We do sneaky shit. I can't and won't tell you that there are not manipulations at play when I speak with you. Can't help it. I've been at this a long, long time. It's become like breathing. But what I can tell you is that we do want the same thing."

Her Southern drawl has ticked up. Murphy makes a mental note of it. Not sure what it means, if it's some sort of tell she lets slip from time to time, or if it's just part of the Agent Margo Darby show.

"Enlighten me, Darby. What do *we* want?"

"Well, I want to keep you alive."

"That's a big one, sure."

"Can always add to that list, if you like. Could work on keeping Dr. Peyton alive. Or, perhaps even your dear, sweet mother." Darby leans back, taking another sip of coffee. "But if you don't feel like you can trust me, then you can trust that it's in my best interest to do everything I can to keep your heart beating."

"Okay, super special agent Darby." Murphy

doesn't trust her at all. Everything Peyton said about her is spot on, but he does like her style. "I do have questions."

"Again, I might have answers. Bear in mind that some of those questions might have answers you'll have to find for both of us."

"Who is Mr. Madness?"

"Wow. Not sure I know that dude. That is kind of a cool name, however."

"Glad you dig it."

"Is it too over the top? Mr. Madness?"

"Prefer not to judge."

Darby presses her lips together with a slight nod. She raises one hand, circling a finger in the air. The door opens. One of the boys in gray enters and she motions him over. She spins her finger around in a few more quick circles, then points down to the floor, clearly communicating that this guy needs to do something they've discussed previously. The man in gray pulls a small, flask-sized bottle of whiskey from inside his jacket and hands it to Murphy.

Murphy recognizes the brand immediately.

The good stuff.

"I understand from Dr. Peyton this is how you prefer to communicate."

Murphy inspects the label. Loves the feel of

this bottle in his hand. Memories flood in. Surprisingly good ones, mixed in with a few he hasn't assigned an emotional tag to yet.

He shared this whiskey with his wife when they worked together at a steak house. Murphy pushes back, shoving that one back deep into the abyss of his mind. This bottle is also the same brand of whiskey he and Peyton shared at the hotel that day in New York. The day he was told his mind was born from two men.

One a highly skilled killer.

The other a kind, smart-ass bartender with a family.

His mind was on fire that day. The confusion still burns inside him most of the time. At that hotel bar they drank this whiskey and spoke with hard words, and even harder hearts, as Dr. Peyton did her best to explain how Murphy's life had been forever changed.

Will this conversation be the same?

Will things become better or worse?

"Peyton said something." Murphy lifts his eyes to Darby. "Right before Mr. Madness stopped by. She said she needed to tell me something."

"Okay."

"Any idea what that might be?"

"None."

Murphy inspects her focused expression. One that gives him nothing. She may have no idea what Peyton wanted to say, or Darby may know exactly what she wanted to tell him.

They lock eyes for a beat that seems to last for hours.

"Now." Darby holds her hand out, asking for the bottle. "Let's pour a little goodness in our coffee and have ourselves a nice chat." Her thin smile and Southern charm are working overtime now. She thumbs back toward the door. "Maybe see if my boys can get us some of that lovely pie."

Super special agent Margo Darby—he isn't sure of her actual title—and Murphy talked for about an hour.

They poured whisky in their coffee.

They ate some pie brought to them by a large mountain of a CIA agent.

Darby just left the room, saying she needed to take care of some things. Some important, time-sensitive items. She also wanted to give Murphy a few moments to let all they discussed soak in.

Murphy can't argue, there's plenty to unpack here.

Darby said she wasn't completely sure how Mr. Madness found him and his mother, but she has some ideas. Of course she does. There were only a handful of people who knew Peyton was coming there to find Murphy.

Three to be exact, according to Darby.

Agent Margo Darby is one. Dr. Peyton, who's slipping in and out of consciousness due to that gunshot wound she sustained while visiting Murphy, and a young agent whose body was found in the trunk of a stolen car.

Darby's eyes glistened a bit when she spoke about the young agent. Tears welled as she talked about how he had worked for her for almost two years now. Just a kid out of The Farm. Could be bullshit. Darby's feelings can more than likely be flipped off and on like a light switch. Feelings manufactured and inserted during training at that same Farm facility. Murphy has come to know that these people can be world-class Shakespearean assholes when called upon.

She said the young agent was killed and then discarded. It's the way the body was left that's curious. It was done in a surprisingly sloppy fashion. Hasty. The body was hidden, but not hidden well. The scene had all the markings of a pro—no readable prints; no eye in the sky video; no trail of breadcrumbs leading anywhere solid—but this pro was someone who was in one hell of a hurry.

Darby's words.

Could mean several things. Could mean the killing was random. Nothing to do with anything. Could mean the body was left to be found as some form of diversion or even a statement. Or—and this is the one Darby is leaning into—the killer didn't want to take the young agent's life, but the killing was viewed as a murder of necessity by someone who knew what they were doing. An unwanted killing by a killer who needed to move fast, for whatever reason.

"Why do you think that?" Murphy asked.

Darby told him about a man named Ernesto. Discussed who Dr. Ernesto was and his involvement with the "other side of the equation" as it's come to be known. How Dr. Ernesto played the same role as Dr. Peyton's but on the darker CIA side that created people like this Mr. Madness, Tinker, and Hiro.

"Like Brubaker?" he asked.

Yes.

Murphy thinks of Mr. Madness. His rage that bubbled under his skin. How his emotions flared when it came to the subject of Brubaker. The man's feelings bounced and pinged off the walls of the diner.

In spite of that, Mr. Madness was there for another reason. He and the other two, Tinker and

Hiro, were there with the intent to kill. Based on what Darby is saying, they were there to kill Murphy and Peyton. Mother would have been a bonus, he supposes. Murphy didn't tell Darby about the affection Mr. Madness expressed for Brubaker. Doesn't know what it means, or how it will be helpful, but Murphy held back that little piece of information when he was talking with Darby on the floor while sipping whiskey-coffee and eating pie.

Might as well keep her in the dark where he can. He knows he needs to hang on to whatever nuggets of gold he might have. God knows she's holding back a shit ton of treasure as well.

"So, you think Mr. Madness is working with this Dr. Ernesto?" Murphy asked.

Darby snapped her fingers, then pointed at Murphy as if he nailed the answer on a game show.

Darby talked about a guy named Agent Irving who worked with Peyton. She said he was a slimy little shit, but she'd never taken him for a turncoat dickhead.

Again, Darby's words.

She went on to say there was nothing in Irving's past that would tie him to Ernesto or the project that produced Mr. Madness. Irving lost a fellow agent not long ago. One he worked with closely. Irving almost lost an eye, and the agent was killed in a slow and brutal fashion during a messy operation that went bad almost immediately. Darby said that after an investigation, some thought signs pointed to sloppy, impulsive work on Irving's part. However, there wasn't enough hard evidence to suspend, fire, or even demote him. He'd been sketchy ever since.

Removed and distant, were the words she used.

Didn't take a genius to understand she likes Irving for the murder of the young agent. Murphy noticed Darby stayed away from talking about Brubaker. Not directly at least. She never even brought up her name. Murphy made another mental note. The personnel file he's keeping in his mind on Darby is getting thicker and thicker by the second. Is she trying to avoid the painful subject of Lady Brubaker when talking to the famously volatile Markus Murphy? Perhaps.

"Give me the protein," Murphy said after he finished his second cup of whiskey-coffee. *"What do you think is happening?"*

"That's why I'm here talking to you," she said.

"You wouldn't be here unless you had something solid."

"Ideas I have. Facts I'm a little light on."

Murphy didn't feel like wasting time punching

each other in the face. There was a game going on there. Always is. One that was being played by both of them. She doesn't trust him, and he does not trust her. A perfect little *you give, I give* dance that was in full swing in that small, beige, shitty room. Murphy gets it. He'd rather cease with all the ceremonial bullshit, but he knows the steps.

"What facts do you have?" he asked.

Darby told him they raided Agent Irving's apartment. Dumped his cell, computers—personal and CIA-issued—along with everything else that could be traced back to him. Social media. Email. Credit cards. Bitcoin transfers. The whole lot.

Murphy knows that doesn't happen simply based on an *idea* of hers. Sure, it starts with a feeling, but she had to have something a little less squishy in order to dig into Irving like she did. She had something solid on him, and maybe, just maybe, those wet eyeballs she was showing off weren't just bullshit CIA tears. She might indeed be a little pissed about the death of that young agent.

"We'll go after him, but that's it," he said.

"We?"

"Me and Mother."

"She's not authorized."

"Neither am I."

Darby took a deep breath, maybe it was two, and then she nodded as she said she needed to talk to some people. She explained that she's a big deal at the CIA but not the biggest deal.

Murphy explained what else he needed in order to take on this task she was asking of him. His needs involved money, guns, and access to information without the usual thick layers of bullshit. He would talk to Darby, and only Darby, until Peyton was well enough to get back into the mix.

Darby didn't argue.

She also did not nod or offer any verbal confirmation, but she listened with her eyes locked on his. She held her phone tight by her knee as if waiting for him to finish laying out his demands before she started making calls.

Words like autonomy were also used by Murphy. Making it clear he does not work for her or the CIA. Said he would take this as far as he felt comfortable. His tolerance for pain is higher than most, but he has no interest in reliving what he went through with Lady Brubaker. It almost killed him, and probably should have.

Didn't share this with Darby, but he wants Mr. Madness and his pals to pay for what he did to Peyton. For what they tried to do to Mother. Murphy felt his blood run like a river of fire as he thought about what could have happened in that diner.

All that could have gone wrong.

There were a lot of people there who had nothing to do with any of this. They were there, much like Murphy and Mother, to enjoy some of the best pie in the universe. They, along with Murphy, Mother, and Peyton, were pretty lucky to a certain extent. One undeniable fact hits him like a sledgehammer—Murphy had frozen when everybody needed him.

He'll never let that happen again.

He can't.

Darby asked him two simple questions. Two Murphy did not want to answer.

"Is your mind stable enough to handle this?" and *"Can you do this?"*

Murphy had taken the bottle of bourbon on his way toward the door while super special agent Darby's two questions hung in the air unanswered. Not sure if he hadn't wanted to give her an answer to chew on, or if he hadn't wanted to think about the truth.

He thinks of the look in Mr. Madness's eyes.

It was the same with Hiro and Tinker. Wild, unstable, and completely void of compassion. He's seen it before in people. Seen it in the mirror too many times to count. Impossible to predict what people like that will do.

One thing is certain, this will not end with a handshake or a calm agreement between rational adults. This ending will be made of blood and lost lives. Murphy would love to avoid the spilling of his own blood, but he knows he has to be better if he wants to lower the odds of the dead being those he cares about.

"On second thought," Murphy said to her, *"I'm going to leave Mother with you."*

"Gee, thanks."

"I'll bring her in once I know more about what's going on." He takes a drink straight from the bottle. *"Still need the guns and money, however."*

Murphy almost made it to the door before Darby snapped her fingers.

"One other thing. Can't believe I almost forgot this part," she said. *"You may want to start with Tinker."*

Murphy turns back.

"Yeah," Darby said. *"We've got him somewhere safe. Just waiting to talk to you."*

MURPHY IS escorted downstairs by one of the CIA's gray suits.

Tinker sits chained in the middle of a poorly lit basement.

This is the somewhere safe Darby talked about.

It's beyond quiet. So quiet there's a buzz. The door shuts behind Murphy as the basement's dim glow grows brighter until it reaches an acceptable level for polite interrogation. The walls and ceiling are padded with soft, two-inch-thick soundproofing material. The floor is rough concrete with scrappy remains of flooring clinging to the rock where it was broken up and yanked away not long ago. A big-mouthed drain sits under Tinker's chair and the room is kept at a cool, bordering on cold, tempera-ture. A hint of ambient music begins playing. You'd have to hold your breath to hear it, but it at least takes a bite out of the dead silence.

All part of the show, Murphy thinks.

Pretty much a waste of time with this guy.

Seems a little cliché to have someone locked up in the basement, but Murphy lets that go for now. He might give Darby some shit later about being too on the nose with this one. To make matters worse, the basement Tinker is chained up in is below the safe house. He was down here the whole damn time. Sitting, waiting while Murphy and Darby snacked on pie, chitchatting, and sipping booze-infused bean juice.

Unbelievable.

Tinker's head jerks giving a wet cough. His head hangs low as if he dropped something important. They have his feet secured together with his torso strapped to a steel chair that's been bolted to the floor. Another chair—leather, comfortable-looking, and unbolted—sits about four feet in front of Tinker. His hands have been left free, but he's seated an arm's length from everything in the mostly empty, small room. A polished table is along the opposite wall, where a pitcher of ice water sits along with a sandwich on a plate.

Nice, Murphy thinks.

Thinker's free hands give the illusion of

freedom with the world just out of his reach. Murphy guesses this is the desired effect, but they also wanted his hands available to look things over, and then provide him this food and water as a mechanism for peaceful negotiation with positive reinforcement. Murphy knows Tinker thinks the same way he does. They share a mind, after all.

That peaceful stuff ain't gonna work.

At least their thoughts should be similar, but without knowing the other side of Tinker's mind, it's impossible to know for sure what's going on it there. Who's in there strolling the fields of Tinker's mind side by side with Murphy? Does he hold a *Mr. Nice Guy* in that skull of his?

He should be so lucky.

Shut it.

"Hey, buddy." Murphy slides over the fat, cushy arm, sinking deep into the vastly superior leather chair across from Tinker.

"Hi, Markus. Pleasure."

"I'm sure." Murphy spins, putting his feet on the floor. "You can call me Murphy. I feel like we already know one another. On a certain level."

"Fair enough." Tinker allows a chuckle that breaks into another hard cough. "Tinker."

Murphy nods.

The cough more than likely stems from the two

slugs he put in Tinker's sternum. The tactical vest he was wearing saved his life, but it didn't come without some painful side effects. He wasn't at the time, but Murphy is now happy he didn't put one in his head. Murphy pulls the bottle of bourbon from his jacket—the one he lifted while talking with Darby—wiggling it side to side so Tinker can see what Murphy considers a peace offering. One he's sure will work.

"No, thank you," Tinker says.

"Really?" Murphy scrunches his nose, then takes a hit off the bottle. "Perhaps I don't know you at all."

"I was sixty days sober when they took me. Did you know that?"

Murphy shakes his head.

"I was at a meeting. In a church. Those assholes grabbed me right out of the parking lot." Tinker's eyes are heavy. He's working hard to get his words out. "They do a lot to try and make you forget that part, ya know? When they take you. How they remove you from your life. Sorry, *extraction of the subject*." Tinker puts his hand out, asking for the bottle. "Tell you what, let me have a snort of that juice. I busted up my sobriety at a strip joint anyway. Care of you taking over my head."

"Sorry." Murphy hands him the bottle.

"Don't be." Tinker drinks. Closes his eyes as it burns down his throat. Tries not to love it. "Having your thoughts, your memories. They're so much fun, ya know? It's a lot to take in but it has been a trip, man. Like an entire skill set has been stuffed into my brain but without any instructions included. No step-by-step on what to do with it all." His distant gaze lifts to Murphy. "Being a skilled killer is an amazing thing."

"Well, I don't like to brag—"

"And yet, so damn sad."

Murphy shifts in the leather. He leans forward, squeezing his hands together. Considers asking for more, but he already knows what Tinker's talking about. Yeah, there's a Mr. Nice Guy in there.

"It was fun for a while, not going to lie. Pretty cool shit if I'm being open and honest here. But I hope they mixed you with someone who helps you, Murphy. I truly do, because after what I've seen lurking inside your mind..." Tinker jams his finger hard to his skull. His chin quivers. "I don't want to see any of this anymore."

Murphy stares, feeling the temperature of his own blood begin to chill.

He's eye to eye with someone forced to share his thoughts. A man who, much like Murphy and Mr. Nice Guy, never asked for any of this. Tinker hands the bottle back. Tinker breathes hard in and out of his mouth, placing his hands on his knees and rocking back and forth as much as the chair will allow him to move. Murphy sees him digging his nails into his thighs, as if attempting to hang on.

"Well." Murphy takes another drink. "It's not all unicorns and blow jobs for me either."

"I bet." Tinker laughs. "Hate you so much."

"Understandable." Murphy clucks his tongue. "I do need to ask you some things. Maybe I can still help you out."

"I only want one thing."

"And that is?"

"I'll wait. Like to hear what you have to say first."

Smart, Murphy thinks. Tinker's shaking slows to a stop. He releases his nails from his thighs.

"You can probably guess the questions, but I'll ask them anyway." Murphy hands him the bottle again. "Do you know a guy called Agent Irving?"

Tinker nods his confirmation.

"Do you know where he is?"

"I know where he was."

"Okay, that's a start." No need for Murphy to confirm Irving's involvement. Darby was spot on about that. "How about a dude named Ernesto? He's a doctor. A scientist. I know you know him in some way, but have you talked to him since you escaped?"

Tinker nods again.

"You want to tell me the one thing you want now?"

"Not yet." Tinker smirks. "Keep going, you're doing well."

"Thanks." Murphy resets. "Did Irving or Ernesto send you and your buddies to kill me?"

Tinker shakes his head no.

"Oh?" Murphy's eyebrows rise.

"No." Tinker takes a drink. "They wanted us to kill all of you."

"You don't say."

"I do say." Tinker hands the bottle back to him.

Murphy presses his lips together. Darby was spot on about all that as well.

"Did a fairly scary CIA woman already talk to you?"

"No." Tinker shrugs. "Some guys in suits locked me up down here, then left me. You're the first one to actually speak to me like a human."

A spike of guilt hits Murphy. Not sure why. He's not responsible for what's happened to Tinker, but he still feels a heavy weight.

"Okay." Murphy claps his hands hard, attempting to snap himself out of it. "Of course, I'm going to need to know where you last saw Ernesto and Irving and all that. But otherwise, I'm fresh out of questions." He takes a drink. "So, let's hear this one thing you want."

Tinker smiles.

He closes his eyes tight. His shoulders draw inward as if he's shrinking. Deflating. His head drops low as his back rises and falls with each labored pull of air. The stillness of the room is hard to take but Murphy doesn't dare disturb it. Then, in a snap, Tinker's head lifts, his eyes pop open wide. His stare is searing. A fire burning in the dark.

Murphy sits up, pushing himself into the cushion of the chair, taken back by Tinker's shift.

"Do you want some water?" Murphy asks. "I can get you something—"

"The one thing. The only thing I want, Murphy?" His voice cracks. "I want to die."

Murphy feels himself peeling away.

"I don't want to be like this." Tinker's eyes are like dark coals. "I don't want you in my head anymore."

Murphy's stomach falls through the floor. Mr. Nice Guy has no answers, nothing to offer in the way of comfort. He looks away, down, anywhere but Tinker's vacant eyes.

"Pull that Glock and finish the job."

"I'll try to help you." Murphy gets up, moving toward the stairs. Desperate to be anywhere but in front of him.

"Help me? Think you've done quite enough, man." Spit flies from Tinker's mouth. "Don't you slither away. You can't let me live like this. Please. I didn't ask for this."

Murphy waits at the door, hoping the gray suits monitoring the room will hurry and let him out.

"You're a virus, Murphy." A larynx-tearing scream. "I do not want your diseased mind."

The door opens and Murphy pushes through.

"Murphy!"

CHAPTER 25

THE ELEVATOR DINGS.

Cool night air greets Mr. Madness and Hiro as they move away from the elevator and out into the dark floor. The parking garage is mostly empty save for a few abandoned vehicles here and there. A homeless man relieves himself in the corner, then screams something about the Lord of Assholes before running away.

Mr. Madness and Hiro each hold their guns low, staying inside the shadows while they let their eyes adjust to their environment. They've said little to one another on the way over to the garage.

Mr. Madness buried deep in his own thoughts.

Hiro keeping to his natural affinity for silence.

This dormant garage is a spot selected by Ernesto. The location was sent to them via the time-bomb text messages they've become accustomed to. Received on the phones that were slipped into their pockets.

Mr. Madness is frustrated with himself. No, it's worse than that. He hates his own weakness. He had a chance to kill them at that diner. They were all there, right in front of him, and he failed.

Why did I hesitate?

He knows why.

Mr. Madness wanted to hear about Brubaker from him. His pulse pounds. He fights to control his breathing. Air pulls in deep, filling his lungs as if he has extra storage for it somewhere. In and out, focused yet calming. The events at the diner strip away pieces of him. So angry for missing that perfect opportunity. He was there. Markus Murphy was there. Peyton, along with Murphy's mother. There's no question that his pathetic—nice quiet Cody—personality stopped Mr. Madness from capitalizing on the opportunity.

He was stopped by an old woman.

The bullet he did fire might have killed the doctor. Dr. Peyton might be dead right now, but he doesn't know. That was what Ernesto wanted, after all, but not what Mr. Madness truly wanted. He doesn't answer to Ernesto. No strings on him.

Mr. Madness checks the time.

Hiro hates himself as well, but his self-loathing is for much different reasons. He left a fallen friend behind. Something he should have never allowed to happen. Tinker was in his grasp and he let him slip away.

The memory cuts through him like a knife. His bones ache like he's been beaten. The searing pain in his shoulder is a constant reminder of what happened. The old woman got a lucky shot on him. At least that's what he tells himself. Deep down he knows he was the lucky one. If her aim was slightly more true, his head would have been removed from his neck. He also knows they will lock down Tinker, if he's even still alive. They will squeeze him for every drop of intel he has inside of him.

Hiro tightens his grip on his gun as his hate turns away from himself.

He wants to kill Markus Murphy. He *needs* to kill him.

Moonlight peeks through the openings that run along the sides of the parking garage. Cuts glowing stalks illuminating only a fraction of the run-down structure. Their feet move as silently as possible through the dirt and slime. Rats scurry. The wind blows a soft whistle outside, mixing in with the other noises of the night.

Mr. Madness can still see his face. Murphy's

face frozen, standing there in the middle of that silly diner among all the other useless sacks of meat and bone. The great Markus Murphy didn't seem so great. Sitting there like a common fool eating pie with his mother and his doctor. The great one needed his mother to save him.

Mr. Madness can't help but laugh.

Hiro throws him a look.

Mr. Madness stops fast. A part of him seizes. He bends at the waist, supporting himself by holding his hands on his knees. He coughs hard. It's as if a cold fist is balling inside his throat. There's a memory of Mother. Of Murphy's mother. It's faint and slippery, but one that has a feeling attached to it. A warm feeling. Mr. Madness screams inside his mind. Begging it to stop.

Brubaker warned him about this.

Hiro cocks his head birdlike watching Mr. Madness seemingly come undone.

Brubaker told Mr. Madness how being face-to-face with Murphy might be problematic. The act of meeting someone who shares a piece of your mind is an insanely odd experience. Even for the strongest of people. Nothing in life would or could prepare you for a moment like it. Mr. Madness needs to be stronger than this. Stronger than he ever imagined. He can't let some half-baked sentimentality stop him from what he wants. He must not hesitate.

Mr. Madness is his own man.

Markus Murphy is not him, and he refuses to be Markus Murphy.

The memory of Mother intensifies.

He needs to stop this part of his shared mind. Must reset his thinking. Cleanse himself of bad thoughts.

Another memory floods in. This one is his, at least he thinks it is. Feels much different. He's in the schoolyard. Bullies are teasing him. They're big and dumb. Pushing him. One slaps him. Calls him a bitch. Mr. Madness remembers the pain actually helped him. He remembers using the pain as a way to change his thinking. To remove himself from himself. The bullies would hurt him, but he'd simply drift away. Inside his mind, at least. They couldn't harm him if he wasn't really there.

Mr. Madness punches his thigh with everything he has.

Mother Murphy is still there.

He hits himself again, only harder. It's not working.

Hiro scans the garage but continues to watch on.

Mr. Madness remembers something else they did to him. He puts his fingers inside his mouth, pinching the meaty muscle under his tongue hard. Mother's face is still present. He squeezes the meat under his tongue harder and harder. Finding a grip is difficult. His fingers slip, fumbling to take hold.

He digs his nails in.

His eyes begin to water. Probably bleeding. Each time her face smiles inside his head he digs deeper, choking on his own spit mixing with blood. His body trembles as the memory fades. His breathing is heavy yet under control. His mouth pulses with pain.

Hiro scrunches his nose. Can't help but think this guy is off his rocker.

A light flickers at the other end of the parking garage.

Hiro nudges Mr. Madness with his hip as he aims his gun toward the light.

Mr. Madness gathers himself.

They both move toward the area where the light came from with guns tacking. Ernesto stands near an abandoned van. Rusted, with at least two flat tires. Ernesto is twitchy. Much more nervous than at the house. Hiro takes note. Mr. Madness takes in all of Ernesto's manic mannerisms. They both watch the doctor's head make quick turns back and forth as he checks the darkness. His eyes darting left and right.

"Where's the other one?" Ernesto asks.

"Something happened." Mr. Madness studies him.

"What? What the hell happened?" Ernesto can barely form a sentence. His teeth gnash. His tongue seems to almost wag. "Okay. Okay. How about Peyton? Where is she? Where is Dr. Peyton?"

"She was shot during the confrontation. I'm not sure where they took—"

"Excuse me, did you say she was shot?" Ernesto's anxiety reaches a new level. "That was not what we discussed. Not at all. Dead is what—"

"I know what we discussed." Mr. Madness's words are cold.

"Murphy was too much for you. Correct? Tell me that's not the case."

"That was not the case." Mr. Madness feels his heartbeat spike again.

"You failed."

"Stop." Hiro grabs Ernesto by the throat. "Not what happened."

Mr. Madness turns his head, thought he heard something move in the darkness. Something in the far corner of the garage. Maybe the homeless guy or a rat, maybe neither. He grips his gun tighter as he studies the dark. The silence creeps back.

Hiro releases Ernesto from his grip.

"What now?" Ernesto coughs out the words. His entire body trembles. "What are we going to do now?"

"Where is Irving?"

Ernesto looks away.

"Where. Is. Agent Irving?"

"He's gone. I don't know where he is. He delivered the location of Dr. Peyton and then he vanished."

"Does the CIA have him?"

Ernesto raises his voice. "I don't know." His words echo across the garage. He lowers his voice immediately, terrified by who might be out there. "But it's a strong possibility."

"So." Mr. Madness thinks. "You have no access to anything useful."

"What?"

"Anything useful." Mr. Madness raises his gun. "You. You are void of use."

"I made you." Ernesto swallows hard. "Let's not forget that."

"Still not of use."

"Your mind is evolving. You're going to need transitional assistance. Guidance and treatment.

There are signs, biological signals, that the procedure might break down over time with you. Both of you. I can help."

"Doubtful."

"Do your eyes bleed?"

Mr. Madness stops. Hiro listens.

"They do, don't they?" Ernesto's speech speeds up. "It was originally thought that was only a side effect. Temporary discomfort. Something that would stop as the healing progressed. But it might be more than that. Let me run some tests."

"No."

Mr. Madness checks Ernesto's pockets, searching for weapons, credit cards, anything really. He pulls out a half-eaten candy bar along with two phones. Similar to the phones Mr. Madness and Tinker found in their own pockets. The ones that transmitted the time-bomb texts to them. He holds the two phones out in front of Ernesto's face.

Dr. Ernesto's eyes pop wide, his face wrapped in confusion. His jaw falls open.

"I don't know where those came from." Ernesto fumbles for the words to try and explain.

Words that do not exist.

"No? Nothing to say?" Mr. Madness hands one of the phones to Hiro.

Both phones buzz at the same time. Hiro looks to Mr. Madness. They check the messages on the screens, then look up to Ernesto.

"What?" Ernesto gasps. "What does it say?"

"In short, it confirms you're of no use."

"What? Who sent that?" All the life drains from Ernesto. "It's from her. Isn't it?"

"It's Brubaker." Mr. Madness can barely contain his excitement.

"That's not possible. It can't be—"

"She wants us to kill you."

Hiro confirms with a nod. They raise their guns.

"No. Wait!" Spit flies from Ernesto's screaming mouth. "You don't understand at all—"

Mr. Madness and Hiro open fire. Ernesto's screams are cut short. His cries still echo, rolling, rippling across the garage as his body flies back, slamming into the rusted van door. Mr. Madness watches his body slide down until it reaches the filthy concrete.

Their phones buzz again.

Their eyes drift down to the screens that cut squares of light in the dark garage. There's a new message. One that will dissolve soon.

Nice job.

Mr. Madness and Hiro look to one another.

Both thinking the same thing. Mr. Madness says it out loud.

"How would Brubaker know—"

"She wouldn't," a woman's voice says.

Mr. Madness and Hiro spin around with guns pointed at the female voice behind them.

"Not Brubaker." A young, attractive woman with a neon-green lizard tattoo on her neck leans against a concrete pillar. She pulls back the wrapper on a hamburger. "That would be me."

Mr. Madness squints. Recognition hits him.

"You were at Ernesto's house."

"I was. As were both of you." A smile in her voice. "Well, you, Mr. Madness, you were in the house. And Hiro here was dutifully scanning the perimeter searching for abnormalities."

"Who are you?"

"I'm the abnormality."

"I'll ask again. Who are you?" Mr. Madness keeps his gun on her.

Hiro does the same.

"I'm a lot like you." She's unfazed by their weapons. "Two minds blended to create a third."

"You escaped the lab?"

She nods.

"I don't remember you." Mr. Madness turns to Hiro. "Do you remember her?"

Hiro shakes his head no.

"You wouldn't, silly. We never had any contact during that confusing time in our lives." She pushes her shoulder away from the pillar, moving toward them. Raises her hamburger to show she has no weapons. "It's not all that important, but I was kept separate from you fellas. Kept with Ernesto."

"Stop."

She obeys, tearing off a bite of burger, then bounces her eyebrows as if waiting further orders.

"I don't understand." Mr. Madness tries to work it through. "If you've been sending the messages..."

"Yes."

"Do you communicate with Brubaker?"

She shakes her head, pressing her lips together with a sympathetic gaze.

"Hate to be the one to tell you this." She chews, then swallows.

Mr. Madness feels his heart jump to the back of his throat.

"Brubaker is dead."

"No." Mr. Madness almost gags on the word. "That's not... That's not possible."

"It is," she says, looking down. "I'm sorry."

Everything inside Mr. Madness shuts down. He lowers his gun, dropping down to his knees. His muscles have given out. Numbness takes over. His eyes see nothing as his thoughts become thick and soft.

"How?" Hiro asks.

"Murphy killed her."

The numbness leaves as quickly as it came on. Mr. Madness's mind sharpens. Dull to razor sharp in a snap. Everything inside him ignites, rolling into a raging synaptic bonfire.

"The good news? Want some good news in all this?" She takes a step closer to them, framing herself perfectly under a shaft of moonlight as she tears off another bite of burger.

Hiro nods. Mr. Madness stares back, seething.

"I know how we can hurt him. I know where the people he cares most about are located."

Mr. Madness rises to his feet. Hiro still has his gun on her.

"Aaaand." She moves toward Hiro, gently pushing his gun down with her hamburger hand. "I know where to find your good buddy Tinker."

Hiro can't hide his smile. The first one in some time.

"Does that interest you boys?"

Mr. Madness gives a single nod.

"Good." Chewing her burger, she pulls a black tactical blade from behind her back.

Mr. Madness and Hiro take a half-step back with guns raised.

"Don't worry." She tears off another burger bite, then flings the wrapper aside. "Need this to cut off Ernesto's hand."

They stare back at her.

"Gotta trust me, boys."

Hiro and Mr. Madness trade looks of absolute confusion.

"Now, listen up, please. This is important. Can't stress this enough." She swallows the last of the burger, giving a satisfied sound. "From here on, everything is going to go really, really fast."

CHAPTER 26

MURPHY STANDS outside the run-down house while cats wander serpentine between his feet.

A headless plastic doll lies sprawled to his right.

A ketchup-stained hamburger wrapper to his left.

Delightful place, Murphy thinks.

He'd surveyed the area—not much around here to survey—then tightened his focus to a fifty-yard radius around the house. Morgues have more activity than this. Not a lot visible on the outside of the house. There's been some slight movement of curtains inside. Minimal, could be the heater or a fan, but enough for someone inside to take a peek if they were being cautious. Murphy saw a shadow move from the front windows toward a side room about thirty minutes ago.

This is the location Tinker gave up.

The last place Tinker said he saw Ernesto and Agent Irving. Murphy finds it hard to believe they are still inside this dilapidated domicile. Doesn't make sense. As smart as they both appear to be, why would they come back here, or stay? Not a smart move. Not one smart people make unless forced. Maybe they had no choice. Maybe Murphy got lucky and arrived before they could make another move. Possible they spotted him and now they are boxed in. Of course, they could be expecting him and are now waiting to pop undesirable holes throughout his body.

One thing is clear, however.

Without question, someone is inside that shitbox of a house.

Murphy reviews what he knows. It's not much, but he does know Mr. Madness and Hiro are out roaming the country freely. More than likely, they are with Ernesto and Agent Irving or an unsavory combination of the two. Doubtful Mr. Madness and Hiro would separate, but they might. Best bet is that Agent Irving is in there. The little movement Murphy has seen inside matches more of the description of him than Ernesto. The *who* of who's inside is easier to piece together, although not completely certain, but it's the goddamn *why* of this thing that is way up in the air.

Why trips you up.

Why fills and clouds the strongest of minds.

Why gets you killed.

Murphy had switched out the candy apple red Porsche for a super nondescript CIA car. Just a shade north of blue in color with dark tint and performance tires. It's an autonomous model with the option to take over the wheel if speed law needs to be broken at the driver's discretion. Theory being an agent can use the travel time to research, study up, and/or recharge but leaves the possibility to go superhero if needed. So, this vehicle can burn when needed, and is dutifully outfitted for tactical play, but looks as boring as your sibling's second husband.

He left the Porsche inside the secured garage near the safe house. Told the men in the gray suits that if he found out there were joy rides taken in his car, he'd gut all of them in front of their families on Christmas Day. He's not sure he'd actually do it, but they must have read the files on him because they turned a whiter shade of pale after he said it.

Those are the moments that make Murphy smile the most.

Mother is a different story. She thinks most things out of Murphy's mouth are trash, disregarding his words as they hit the airwaves. To say she was not happy with Murphy's decision to leave without her is the understatement of the century. There was an avalanche of profanity and personal assaults, but Murphy knows some caring was buried deep in the center of it all. At least he hopes there was some caring in there.

She's always been fairly brutal with her love.

Mother saw him freeze at the diner. She, more than anyone, knows what happened and what is possible out in the world. *A whole lot of horrible,* she said. She almost begged him to take her along, but he knew she needed to stay right where she was. Mother doesn't need his protection. But still, Murphy can't let anything happen to her. He's been the cause of too much *horrible* already.

Needs to cut back where he can.

He told her she needed to stay and look after Peyton. Complete bullshit. Mother saw through it, of course. There was ample medical staff and armed CIA goons at the house that was tricked out to be a CIA fortress. Murphy tried to go with the idea that Peyton needed a friendly face in the crowd, though everyone knows Mother does not qualify. Regardless, Murphy left her at the safe house with Peyton and in the loving arms of the CIA.

She'll forgive him. Someday. Maybe.

But only if whoever is inside this cat-infested shitbox doesn't kill him first. Darby had made good on her word. Set him up with the guns and money he requested. Murphy wasn't sure what he needed, but he's found that in this jagged mess of a life guns and money never hurt.

More is vastly superior to less.

He was also granted full access to all transportation the CIA has at its disposal. He was given some encrypted cards, and a thick roll of cash for those seedy individuals who still prefer the anonymity of cash. They gave him plenty of ammo for his favorite Glock, along with a Ka-Bar tactical blade, which he has strapped to his person, and a rubber-gripped assault Mossberg he has secured in the trunk.

He's also been given a handful of injectors with a powerful sedative.

Small, the size of a quarter, they can be jammed directly into a subject or flung like tiny Frisbees from a somewhat safe distance. They will plunge knockout juice into a person at the speed of a hypodermic needle upon impact. Murphy has used these before. Hell, they've been used on him before. Both recently. He regrips his Glock. Runs through his options again. He's thought through the possibilities.

Murphy sees no need to dance around the issue a second longer.

Running full speed toward the front of the house, he squeezes off two shots, blowing out the glass of the picture window a fraction of a second before he launches himself. Tucking, turning his shoulder slightly as he clears the window, he lands, rolling on the floor and then up to standing position. The rubber soles of his boots grip the floor as his feet land. He feels blood trickle down his arms and back, burning from the slices he caught from the razor-sharp shards during entry.

A slick, olive-skinned man rushes toward him with a gun raised.

Murphy levels his weapon, holding up a flat palm with his free hand, asking for moment before the shooting starts.

"Irving." Murphy speaks in as calm a voice as he can find. "Agent Irving?"

Agent Irving nods.

Murphy looks him over, not sure he believes what he's seeing. Irving's clothes are torn and bloodied in places. His eyes are dark. Beads of sweat run down from his hairline, and his dress shirt is soaked around his loose-hanging tie. But that isn't what has Murphy's heart skipping beats.

There's something covering Irving's mouth.

The entire lower part of his face, actually. It runs below his nose, under his chin and along his jawline, wrapping around the back of his neck. It's made of a hybrid material used almost solely by the military. A breathable, flexible material but stronger than steel.

Murphy's seen these before.

It was a hostage situation. The cartels use these "closers" on kidnap victims or with people they don't want exercising loose lips, but who they don't want to kill just yet. The device wraps around the mouth and jaw, keeping a person quiet, but allows them to breathe and has a setting that allows for food and drink for brief periods of time. More effective than classic cloth. Very hard to remove, more humane, and less permanent than cutting out a tongue. Although, if you try to remove it and get the code wrong, the device will snap the jaw off your face. Again, difficult to remove, but not impossible.

Murphy can do it, but Agent Irving will have to trust him. That might be asking a lot given all that has happened. Making a quick scan around the house, he searches for something. A way to communicate. A pen and paper, something for Irving to write on. Anything. A way to get answers without guns and hard looks.

The house is empty save for a beat-up couch and table that sit along the wall. There are dirt rings clinging to the walls, perhaps marking where things once hung. Outlines buried in the layers of dust, paper-sized squares, on the lone table next to the couch. And small circular imprints in cheap rugs where various tables or chair legs once sat. There's a power cord still plugged into the wall. This place was cleaned out in a hurry. As if someone knew a storm was coming and they needed to evacuate immediately.

Something catches Murphy's eye.

In front of the couch, placed in plain sight, is a platinum digital storage device. From where Murphy stands, it looks to have a biometric reader along the front. Seems to require a palm print to access. He thinks of the roof in New York above Central Park. Thinks of how he took Agent Thompson's eyes to access a different biometric reader.

Irving snaps his fingers at Murphy, getting his attention. He's holding up a cell phone, moving it wildly back and forth, then stabbing it frantically with his finger. Murphy nods. Irving flips the phone over. On the back, there's a wide strip of yellow tape with the name MURPHY written in black marker across it.

"Put it on the floor," Murphy says, keeping his Glock pointed at Irving's head. "Then kick it over to me."

The phone spins and skips its way over. Murphy stops it with his foot. The screen is dark and dead, waiting for communication to bring it to life. He looks up to Irving. The man is terrified. He's fighting hard to seem like he's keeping it cool, but it's not working. His gun shakes while pointed in the general direction of Murphy.

Irving holds out a hand, asking for a moment, then motions that he is going to place his hand into his pocket.

Murphy nods permission.

Irving pulls out another phone that's identical to Murphy's, only the yellow strip on the back has IRVING written across in black marker. A cat meows, rubbing against Murphy's leg. He almost shoots it but shoos it aside instead.

"I can get that thing off your face."

Agent Irving shakes his head no.

"I can. It's not easy, but I can take it off and we can talk like civilized folk." Murphy points his toe toward the phone on the floor. "I don't know what the hell all this is about, or who did this to you, but I can help you." Murphy swallows, forces a disarming smile. "Will you let me help you?"

Irving keeps his gun on him. Eyes floating. Distant.

Murphy's losing him.

"Look, man. I was driving around eating pie before all this shit. Things weren't perfect but I was doing okay, ya know? Didn't ask for any of this, believe me, but some people just can't let other people be happy. I'm guessing those happiness killers are people you know pretty well, right?"

Irving's phone buzzes in his hand.

Murphy's phone vibrates, bouncing on the floor.

Their lock eyes. Breathing stops. Agent Irving starts to raise the phone to read the message.

"Wait," Murphy calls out. "Don't look at the screen yet. Whatever it says, whatever asshole set this up, we can work this out. Me and you."

Irving's stops just shy of bringing the screen all the way up to eye level. His stare is a thousand yards out into nothing, neither looking directly at the phone nor at Murphy. Murphy knows this moment is a delicate dance along a razor wire.

"Did someone bring you here?" Murphy asks.

No response. Irving stands staring back at him

like a blank slab of meat.

"Hey," Murphy barks. "Give me something, man. I'd love to ask you some questions. Easy ones. Give me a head shake or a nod. Simple yes-or-no stuff. Then, we'll check whatever the hell is on those phones together. At the same time. That sound reasonable?"

Agent Irving's eyes shift to meet his. Murphy nods, hoping for a connection.

"Okay." Murphy takes a deep breath, lowering his gun. "Did someone bring you here?"

Agent Irving stares—a beat that seems to last forever—then lowers his gun as he nods a yes.

"Cool. We're doing good here. Was it Mr. Madness? Was it Hiro?"

Shakes his head no.

"Who, then?" Murphy lets slip out, then waves off the question. "Sorry. How many people brought you here?"

Agent Irving holds up the phone, raising his index finger.

"One?" Murphy's mind fumbles. "Ernesto?"

Head shake.

"Was Ernesto here?"

A nod.

"Is Ernesto alive?"

No.

The phones buzz again.

"Did this person give you these phones?"

Panic tears roll down Irving's trembling face as he begins to lift the phone again.

"Wait." Murphy bends down to pick up his phone. "You're doing great. Thank you so much. But—"

Agent Irving snaps his fingers again at Murphy. His eyes direct Murphy with an ever-so-slight tilt of the head toward the far wall. Murphy squints. There's a tiny red dot above the couch just below a dirt ring. Barely larger than a pinprick, but there's no mistake that it's a camera. The *one* who did this is watching.

Murphy nods back to Irving, knowing he's fresh out of time.

The phones buzz again.

Murphy picks up the phone, then stands up. He grips his gun. An apologetic stare is shared between them. They each look at the screens of their phones.

Murphy reads: *If you can get that off him, great. But if you kill him quick...*

Murphy lowers his phone. Fights for focus. Fumbles through the forest fire raging inside his mind. Whoever is pulling the strings knew he'd come here. Wanted him to come here. Murphy looks across the room. He needs to know what Irving knows. Time is a luxury Murphy does not have.

The phone slips away from Agent Irving's fingers.

Face pale, shaking, he raises his gun.

Murphy whips his arm to the right, firing multiple shots into the wall. Blasts out the area where he saw the camera. Bullets zip past Murphy as he dives, rolling clear. Agent Irving turns, taking aim, spit flying from his mouth as he screams.

Murphy fires a single shot. Irving's shoulder explodes, almost separating from the body. Irving's gun bounces to the floor. Springing forward, Murphy knocks Irving's gun away, sending it spinning into the far corner.

Murphy jams an injector into Irving's neck. His body thrashes once, then his eyes flutter and fade as his body goes limp. It's not as powerful as ketamine but it's not Tylenol PM either.

Murphy hopes like hell the combination of the gunshot wound and the injection doesn't kill him. He needs answers from Agent Irving. He'll never be free of this if he can't—

The phone buzzes again.

There's a whirring. A mechanical grinding coming from Agent Irving's jaw.

"No. No, no, no."

Murphy looks to the phone.

Cute. Can't have Irving talking to you.

Irving's head twitches. Jerking down until his chin is lowered into his chest as the tension from the "closer" device ratchets tighter and tighter. Murphy closes his eyes. He knows the horrible sounds that will soon follow. The soft cracks. The cutting of meat and muscle. Murphy shoves himself back with his heels as he hears Irving's temporomandibular joints pop. If the code isn't entered, it won't be long until the device will sever his head from the spine. A code Murphy does not have.

Blood will blanket the floor.

Murphy takes some comfort in the fact Agent Irving won't be conscious for his horrible death. Whoever is out there knew the possible outcomes of this situation they created. Murphy turns it over and over in his head. Even if Irving had killed Murphy, Irving was going to die. This person rolled the dice thinking maybe Irving could take Murphy out, but if he didn't, Irving dies either way. Or at the minimum, Irving keeps Murphy busy. Distracted. Keeps Murphy away from—

Another message buzzes through to the phone.

We've found a nice, safe house to visit.

CHAPTER 27

Margo Darby is a little over a mile away from the safe house.

She'll park in a garage a few blocks north after circling the area around the house, checking for tails and obvious abnormalities. Been a while since she was a field agent, but the moves are still the same. Those types of lessons learned are not quickly forgotten. This routine is good, but it is less than perfect. You can check a location a thousand times and nothing will be there, then find the devil himself lurking in the shadows the one thousand and first time you look.

The cameras in the garage are monitored by AI, with a rotating team of human CIA to spot-check. The CCTV feed is disabled when needed. Meaning when Darby enters and leaves the garage.

Also, not out of the question for some footage to simply go away. From the garage, it's a short walk down a short street past some casual shopping and dining on the verge of bankruptcy. Then it's another fifty yards down a back alley that spills out into a lower-middle-class neighborhood that's long past its prime.

Perfect for a CIA safe house.

The house isn't completely secluded but there's enough space between the homes to avoid prying eyes. Also helps that four out of the six houses on the street are abandoned. The CIA owns the other two. Homeless wander the streets, sleeping on porches and occasionally swatting at things that aren't there. The few people who do live nearby are hardworking, pushed-to-the-limit families who keep to themselves, their doors and curtains pulled tight and mouths closed. The house next to the safe house has been deserted for months. The bulky lock from the real estate agent still hangs on the front door. Murphy had made a comment about envying the agent's unbridled optimism.

Darby hopes Murphy found something at that house Tinker gave up.

Hopes he finds anything, really.

He hasn't checked in since he arrived. She didn't expect a play-by-play from the man, but she does wish this split-head asshole would throw her a bone. Even though she's been at this a long time, she still gets the jitters at times like this. The unknown can be a constant in this line of work, but it still gets to her from time to time. And this time, there's a metric shit ton of unknown that can and will cause a lot of pain and suffering.

She's received word from the safe house that Dr. Peyton is awake and alert.

Great news.

Murphy's mother is being a complete pain in the ass.

Expected.

And Tinker has shut down completely. Nonresponsive. Won't talk and is refusing to eat.

"Come on, Murphy," she mutters to herself as the autonomous car turns the corner for her last pass of the area before entering the garage.

She's looked over everything she has available on the way over. Scanning emails. Pictures. Video footage. There's nothing new, but she keeps at it, hoping to see something she or other agents have missed before. Brubaker is still nonresponsive, lying in a heavily guarded room at a military hospital. Darby just got off a call updating her status. Vitals are good, but she's still out like a light.

Darby can't imagine what's going on in Brubaker's mind.

She can't imagine what's going on inside Murphy's head either.

"Messing with shit that shouldn't be messed with," she mutters.

Darby's been talking to herself more and more since this all started. Maybe she needs someone to work on her head as well. Ever since she walked the war-torn remains of Central Park, she's felt an odd pushing and pulling from inside of her. The walk-through of Murphy's firefight in Montauk didn't help. This entire project—calling it simply a case seems ridiculous—is nothing she's ever experienced before. She's grateful for the opportunity, of course. This is one that could push her up and into the stratosphere at the agency if she nails it. But if she fails? She shoves that thought out of her head with both hands.

Her car stops at a light near the parking garage. A message pops up in the left corner of the windshield telling her she's clear to pull into the garage and park.

"Thanks," she tells the car, not sure why.

A whispered zip hits the security glass of her back window. Doesn't penetrate, but the pounding thump gets her attention. She's under fire.

Darby slams down the gas, taking control of the car.

The reinforced steel of the driver's door plunks and pops. The fire she's taking is rapid. Loud. Closer. There are at least two gunmen—one elevated sniper, one on the ground with an assault weapon.

"Shit." Darby drops down to the floorboard, pulling her gun. "Drive," she barks at the car.

A calm, artificial voice asks for a location.

"Who gives a damn. Idaho. Fast." Her training cuts through the fog. "Protocol ninety-nine. Pedal down."

The car jerks forward as the CIA-enhanced automation kicks in. Darby checks her weapon, hoping the zero-to-sixty estimates she's been given on this car are correct.

Another two quick zips blow out the rear tires.

The car jerks hard to the left, sending the car into the beginning of a spin. The calm, artificial voice says something about stabilization failure. Darby grits her teeth, bracing herself however she can.

The voice says something about impact.

Another vehicle slams into the passenger side with incredible force. Darby's sight goes white, then dissolves into vibrating globs of blurs and smears. She feels blood drip down her face. The car skids, tires screeching to a stop. Emergency protocols are kicking in. The agency was called the second the first bullet hit the glass.

Whoever is out there probably knows that.

Darby pushes herself up, fighting through the swirling slush of her mind. The pounding in her head. The pooling blood in the floorboard.

They'll want to finish the job fast.

She digs her nails into the leather seat, pulling up, her weapon ready. Through the ringing in her ears, she focuses in on the sound of rapid footsteps. She silently counts to three.

"Open driver door now."

The door flings open, framing a small man lumbering toward the car with an assault rifle. Darby opens fire. Her aim and sight are a mess. She points in his general direction—hoping any civilians are clear—pulling the trigger.

As the gunman wilts to the concrete, Darby hears sirens wail in the distance.

Her eyes flutter closed.

Grip on her gun goes slack.

Darby slides back down to the floorboard.

CHAPTER 28

Murphy tries calling Mother again.

Nothing.

He orders the car to try the emergency line at the safe house.

No answer.

Calls Darby one more time. Straight to voicemail.

Murphy has the car pegged at over ninety most of the way. When he switched over to manual mode, he hit a hundred-plus on a several-mile stretch of straight road. He'll be there soon.

Soon might not be good enough.

They told him some rather lengthy CIA bull-shit about using security protocols and parking at a garage a few blocks from the safe house. Going through an alley and blah, blah, freakin' blah.

Murphy will be pulling the car up front today, thank you.

How is it possible all communications to the safe house are dead?

Sure, they might be able to jam cell signals. Certainly, if the CIA wasn't expecting it. But the emergency line is an old-school hard line. Murphy runs through the logic progression. If whoever is doing this knows the CIA—and they appear to be well-educated so far—then they could be savvy enough to cut or disrupt the hard line.

Murphy could do that.

Did it in Oklahoma about four years ago. He and another killer for dollars had to go in strong. Had to take out a similar safe house tucked away outside Oklahoma City. Small, nondescript, but the house held some homesick KGB, along with a wayward CIA agent, who needed to have their mouths closed forever. Coms were cut. Door was smashed in. Bodies removed like pulling weeds.

Could Mr. Madness and Hiro be so dialed into Murphy's experiences that they could pull out that skill and execute it?

Seems unlikely.

Not impossible, but that is a second-level type of task that requires detailed work and the knowledge to adapt if faced with unknowns. A technical skill. Far different than a peeling away of morals or softening a view on killing. More than aiming a gun or throwing a punch.

Are they evolving?

Are they adapting faster than I did?

Are they digging deeper and deeper into my mind?

Traffic is thick up ahead. Cars backed up for miles with emergency vehicles parked in the distance. Murphy checks the onboard navigation. An animated icon that resembles a car wreck is shown near the parking garage. The garage where he is supposed to obey the CIA security protocols for the safe house.

That can't be random. No way that's a coincidence.

"What's the wreck up ahead?"

A few soft clicks. "Police reporting shots fired." A few more clicks. "Agency alert seconds ago. Agent Margo Darby down—"

"Reroute to the original destination." Murphy checks the load on his Glock. Closes his eyes, searching for the correct combination of words to use. "Ignore stated traffic laws. Markus Murphy confirmed. Verification code... Hard Scramble Six, Six, Alpha, Delta, Four."

"Verification accepted."

"Notify the agency. Safe house breached."

"Message to be sent." The car's voice pauses as the wheel turns hard, accelerating in a new direction. "Team is deployed. Will arrive in thirteen minutes."

"Jesus." Murphy slams the dashboard. "How fast can we get there?"

"At the current rate of speed, our estimated time to destination is ten minutes."

"Fuck that." Murphy grabs the wheel, slams down the gas. "Show me the route."

A digital map spreads, overlaying across the windshield, taking up most of the passenger side. Faint, but enough to see the map while still being able to view the road somewhat safely. Murphy jerks the wheel left then right, weaving in and out of traffic. His fingers grip the leather until his knuckles pop. Tires scream. Horns blare. His eyes bounce between the road and grids of streets digitally laced on the windshield.

"There." He taps a street corner on the map a few blocks north of the pulsing blue dot destination. "Reroute there."

The yellow line alters, showing a new path. The estimated time changes to eight minutes.

Murphy knows he can do it in four—five max.

Knows he can sprint full out to the house

in one.

The car jumps as Murphy cuts the wheel hard, pushing the front tires up onto the sidewalk. He lays on his horn. People dive left and right. Screaming, scrambling to get out of the way, flying clear of the speeding bullet of a vehicle. Murphy stomps the gas to the floor, holding loosely to the fading line between control and chaos. The back of the car fishtails as he whips into a wide turn.

A series of black and white patrol cars race past, headed in the other direction as if he wasn't there.

Murphy's call into the agency notified local law enforcement that his car was untouchable. A blind spot within the law. Murphy tells the car to have the police close off a three-block radius around the safe house. The car cuts through someone's yard. A fence explodes into chunks and splinters as Murphy's car rams through, jumps a curb, catches some air, and lands in the middle of a neighborhood street.

Murphy stands on the brakes, skip-skidding to a stop.

Flying out from the car, he pops the trunk, holstering his Glock behind his back. He grabs the Mossberg assault shotgun inside the trunk that rests next to the platinum digital storage device he took from the house with Irving. Breaking into a sprint, Murphy charges hard down the street toward the safe house.

The sun shines bright.

The air is cool and crisp.

His legs pump like pistons. Acid runs through his veins, his lungs breathe fire.

Nothing seems out of place at the safe house. There are two cars in the driveway, but those CIA specials were there before. Nothing parked in front of the house. Nothing looks or sounds out of place. Murphy didn't get a full view inside the house earlier, only parts of it, but enough to know the general layout.

It's a two-story home with a basement. If he's lucky, he can get access through the second story and work his way down. Attempting to kick in the front door might get him and others inside killed. If Mr. Madness and friends are inside, they might be waiting for him. Maybe they aren't even there yet.

Murphy pulls up, slowing down to a jog. He tries calling one more time.

Nothing.

If they cut the lines and jammed the phones, then they are close to the house, if not inside. He looks toward a dilapidated home next door. One he knows has been abandoned for some time. Darby made a point of telling him how secure the safe house was in this forgotten neighborhood. Weeds and grass have grown tall and out of control in the front yard, which has a weathered, beaten-down For Sale sign off the sidewalk. He zeros in on the door. A detail that's out of place. There was a lock on the door before. A bulky one with a bio reader left by a real estate agent.

The lock is gone.

A curtain moves ever so slightly. He's been made.

Murphy races to the front door of the safe house. He waves his hands wildly at the door for the security cameras to see. Hopefully they won't shoot him. He beats his fists on the door. There's no telling what Mr. Madness and Hiro have planned next door. Time is up.

One of the CIA gray suits opens the door. Murphy—never thinking he'd be glad to see these assholes—shoves his way through, slamming the door behind him.

"The house is blown." Murphy owns the room. "All coms have been cut. Darby was attacked. Bad guys are next door. Lock this shitbox down."

The Gray Suits scatter. Training and protocols kicking in as if a cord had been pulled.

"I need a gun." Mother stands next to him.

"You certainly do." Murphy snaps at a passing Gray Suit. He holds up two fingers, then presses both fingertips against the barrel of the Sig Sauer the CIA agent holds.

Murphy turns back to Mother. "You still mad at me?"

"Never stop being pissed at you."

The Gray Suit comes back with two Sig Sauers and a handful of loaded magazines. Murphy shoves a gun in Mother's hand along with two mags. Mother takes the gun with a motherly sneer.

"I'll deal with your bitch-ass later." She checks the load.

"Peyton?"

"Alive, but shitty." Mother pushes her chin toward a room behind her.

Sidestepping a Gray Suit who's rushing up the stairs, Murphy moves fast into a small room, where he finds Peyton is sitting up in bed. Dragging her feet over the side, she carefully lands them on the floor as her teeth grind. With one arm in a sling, she pops some pills with her good arm.

Murphy raises his eyebrows. "You good?"

"Amazing." She holds her hand out. "Give me a goddamn gun."

Murphy tosses the Sig and an extra mag onto the bed next to her.

Two shots crack upstairs. A dull thump sounds.

"Here we go." Murphy puts a hand on the doorknob. "This door opens without a knock? Keep firing until they or you are dead."

Peyton gives a half-hearted thumbs-up as he shuts the door.

Murphy checks the corners of the living room, leveling his shotgun on the stairs. A young Gray Suit with his gun raised takes what cover there is near the front door. Murphy knows Mr. Madness and Hiro can come at them from any and every angle. He motions for a young agent to move clear of the window. There's a faint sniff of gunpowder from upstairs. The entire house has fallen into a chilly silence. The drops of quiet that fall before chaos.

Murphy's fingers tingle. There's an itch to his skin.

They're here. He can feel Mr. Madness's disease. Hiro's cold brutality is with him.

Still, there has to be more than just the two of them. They'd need a small team. Not impossible, but unlikely they could take on Darby and make it back here in time to stage a full-on assault on a CIA safe house. Not out of the question, but unlikely even for those who share Murphy's mind. One helluva big bite for those two to choke down.

Murphy's thoughts jump to the night at the house in Montauk.

Thoughts race to the one who came down the stairs. He wasn't like the others. He was weaker than the rest. He was deformed physically, possibly mentally. Peyton said some of them turned out like Mr. Madness. Some like Hiro. One like Lady Brubaker. Then there were some who weren't as strong. The lesser ones of the pack. Not without utility, but not first-string starters in the big game either. Darby, Peyton—even the late Agent Thompson—didn't know for sure how many split-heads there were out there in the world.

Murphy glances to the door that leads downstairs to the basement where Tinker is secured. Somewhere in all this, Mr. Madness and Hiro will make a move. They want Murphy, but they also came here to free their friend.

God knows what else they want.

The front door cracks. The walls shake.

Something slams into the door. As if an unhinged bull wants inside. They're trying to ram their way in. A bold move. Questionable way to go. Won't be easy to bust through, maybe impossible; the CIA doesn't put in doors the big, bad wolf can easily blow down.

Maybe that's not the point.

They found a weak point upstairs to exploit; now they want to control the front. Even if they can't breach the door, they want them to know they are there. Close off an exit. Murphy guesses they sealed off the garage somehow, the only rear exit.

The door cracks again.

Murphy looks to Mother. She readies her Sig, stepping up beside him. He motions to the young Gray Suit near the door. They lock eyes. Murphy points to the door. The Gray Suit swallows hard, looking like he'd rather do anything else. He gives a nod as his trembling hand moves toward the bio reader to the left of the door. His other hand hovers over a square metal button just above the reader.

"Markus Murphy," a voice booms from upstairs.

Mr. Madness.

"Do it," Murphy bark-whispers.

In a single move, the Gray Suit scans his palm and jams the button with everything he has. The door flies open. Two men in tactical gear stand with a battering ram pulled back, ready to strike at the door again. Faces stunned and blank. Eyes dull and weak. Murphy and Mother open fire, cutting them to shreds.

"Shut it." Murphy pumps his shotgun.

The Gray Suit punches the button again. The

door slams shut. They hear the sound of the bodies falling outside.

"Come on down, little Miss Madness," Murphy booms back. "I can do this shit all damn day."

The house returns to its previous eerie silence.

Murphy rushes over, checking the windows. Clear outside save for the two sacks of meat bleeding out on the porch. He leans down, speaking into the ear of the Gray Suit.

"Talk to me," Murphy says. "We have anyone at the back?"

Gray Suit shakes his head no.

"How many upstairs?"

Gray Suit holds up two fingers.

A sound spins them both around. A body in a bloodied gray suit rumbles down the stairs. Glides down, sliding over the steps, then lands in a heap near Mother. The agent has been shot twice. Killed and his body tossed down the stairs. A clear message sent that cannot be misunderstood. Mother's body begins to shake. Not from fear. From rage.

Gray Suit now holds up only one finger.

"Move to the basement. They'll go for their buddy."

Gray Suit scrambles down into the basement with his Sig ready. Murphy looks to Mother. She regrips her gun, taking in a deep breath. Murphy readies his shotgun. The Gray Suit on the floor in front of them stares back with eyes wide and lifeless. What's left of his blood seeps away from his body.

A clunk from upstairs. Something thumps, rolling down the stairs.

Murphy and Mother take aim.

A severed head tumbles, bouncing, skipping every other step. Removed at the neck, the head comes to a rolling stop near Murphy's feet. Mother holds her mouth. Holds back the tears flooding her eyes.

Murphy stares, dialing in, recognizing the man's face. It's the large mountain of a CIA agent who brought him and Darby pie in the basement. Another body comes sliding down the stairs. The suit soaked in blood. Jacket up where a head should be.

Mr. Madness has come undone, much like Brubaker, Murphy thinks.

Mother moves toward the stairs, gun raised. She's had enough.

Murphy makes a quick scan over the headless body. Something is off. This is the body of a man with an average build. The suit doesn't fit. Loose, far too big. The body does not match the head of the man Murphy knows. Murphy reaches for Mother, but she pulls away from his outstretched fingers.

The headless body pulls the jacket down. Mr. Madness twists at the foot of the stairs, flipping onto his back. He squeezes off two blasts.

Mother's body jolts, flying backward.

The impact spins her around, sending her into the wall. Everything inside Murphy freezes. The world slows. As if life was running a quarter of its normal speed. He watches Mother slide down the wall, spreading her blood like a broad brush as she reaches the floor.

No! Murphy screams inside his head.

It's happening again. This feeling, identical to what happened at the diner.

Mr. Madness pushes himself up from the floor, shedding the ill-fitting jacket.

Murphy stands like a statue, watching him as he gets to his feet. His mind rages, pleading for his arms to raise his shotgun and remove Mr. Madness from the planet. His body fails him. Disobeying every signal fired off from his burning mind.

Mr. Madness cocks his head, looking Murphy over.

His knowing stare bores through Murphy. The woman with that magnificent green lizard on her neck said there was a possibility of this happening. The possibility of the great Markus Murphy shutting down. Again. She's been right about everything so far. *Crashing,* she called it. And it's happening right before his eyes.

Mr. Madness loves it. Loves that he's here to witness the end of Murphy. He takes it in, wants to soak in the moment. Embracing how fragile Murphy is at this snapshot in time. It's almost impossible to accept how helpless he seems.

This man.

This man who tried to take her. Who tried to take and discard the love of Brubaker. Mr. Madness would cherish all of her with endless, effortless gratitude.

Hiro walks down the stairs.

Murphy can only watch as his large frame swallows the stairway. Hiro steps over the severed head and body that lie at the foot of the stairs as if they were spilled milk. Mr. Madness says something to Hiro, but Murphy can't make out the words. Hiro stares blankly at Murphy, then raises his gun while going toward the basement door. Going after his friend.

Mr. Madness turns back to Murphy.

Ponders the moment, then slips his gun behind his back. He shows an ever-so-slight crack of a smile as he pulls a knife from his ankle. A Ka-Bar. Murphy knows this type of blade well, therefore so does Mr. Madness. Murphy knows he wants to feel this. Wants to take in the unmistakable feeling of taking Murphy's life with a blade. Tactile. Primal. The desire to remember this moment forever burns deep inside of Mr. Madness. He so badly wants to hold on to the moment he removes Murphy's life from him. The moment Mr. Madness kills the alpha.

Murphy looks over the blade as it inches closer and closer.

Raise your shotgun, asshole!

Do something!

Gunshots ring out from the basement. Murphy knows Hiro has already won.

Mr. Madness steps closer to Murphy. Holds the large knife gently, like an egg. Playful.

Murphy's mind is reduced to globs of misfiring emotions failing to connect. Watching, he takes in everything as if it's happening to someone else. Front row seat at a movie that will not produce a feel-good ending.

The shotgun slips from his fingers. Accepting the ending as eventual.

Mr. Madness watches the gun fall to the floor. Almost disappointed he's being denied the fight he's imagined. The one he dreamed of while waiting upstairs. No matter. He grips the knife tight. Ready.

He glances toward Mother. She's balled up by the wall. Blood starting to pool. She doesn't have long. A new sound enters Murphy's mind.

A voice.

One that cuts through the collection of endless nothingness.

One he hasn't heard before, or that he has forgotten. The voice isn't his own. It is not the voice of Mother, Noah, or even Kate. It's two voices. Tangled, woven together, forming a single soul-melting sound. Angelic voices wrapped and coiled into one.

The combined sound of the girls fills his mind.

He's never experienced this sound inside his head. New, yet achingly familiar at the same time. His splintered mind has blocked the memory of how wonderful they sound. Their laughter as he played with them. The joyous sound of a child discovering a new world. It's amazing. A staggering memory of auditory bliss. Perhaps one his mind protected him from before.

Murphy's fingers tingle. Electricity rips through his veins.

Mr. Madness stands inches from him. Blade raised. Smile big and wide.

Murphy clucks his tongue.

Mr. Madness stops. His chest tightens as his sick smile fades. Confusion surges. There's a new look in Murphy's eyes. A light now shines in eyes that were dark and lost only seconds ago.

Murphy grabs a fistful of Mr. Madness's hair.

Lifts up onto his toes and then pulls down fast, yanking Mr. Madness down hard using all the force and strength he has. Murphy wraps his free hand around the clenched fist that holds the knife. Holds the blade steady, moving it up and pushing through Mr. Madness's throat.

Murphy releases.

Mr. Madness stumbles back as his fingers slide and fumble at the blade. Fighting to pull it free from his neck as his fingers slip helplessly off the handle. Blood pours down the white shirt and loosened tie. His eyes spread wide. Gurgling nonsense tumbles out from his lips as Mr. Madness falls to his knees.

Murphy grabs the shotgun and rushes to his mother's side. Her face is pale. Her body shakes and twitches. There's a pulse. Weak, but there's a sign of life.

He checks his phone. No signal. Still jammed.

He can't count on when the CIA will arrive. Murphy runs to the basement door. As he moves down the stairs, he can hear Tinker yelling. He's upset. His voice crackles. Sounds like angry pleading.

"No," Tinker yells. "No more."

Hiro stands by his friend. The body of the gray suit lies at his feet. Hiro's face is wrecked with an expression of hopelessness. Tinker's eyes are full of tears, his cheeks flushed red. The same lost man Murphy talked to before. A man who has given up. Hiro sees Murphy as he reaches the last step.

Murphy levels his shotgun on Hiro. Hiro raises his gun on Murphy.

"It's over," Murphy says. "We can all walk out of—"

"No. Absolutely not." Spits flies from Tinker's lips. "Do it, Hiro. End all this."

Hiro shakes his head no as tears roll down his face.

"Do it, man. Please," Tinker begs. "This only ends one way. You know it too. I don't want this. The thoughts, the memories of death, the fucking weight of all the suffering we've caused."

"Put the gun down, Hiro," Murphy presses. "He's wrong. I can help—"

"Help?" Tinker yells. "Is that a serious statement?"

Hiro keeps his gun on Murphy but his eyes on Tinker.

"This is the rest of our lives." Tinker's heads drops down. "I can't do this."

"Come on, man." Murphy moves slow and easy toward them. "Let's talk."

Tinker looks up to Hiro. "You can't do this either."

Hiro nods as his stare slips over to Murphy. Cold. Empty.

"No!" Murphy screams, rushing toward him.

Hiro turns fast, firing a shot between Tinker's eyes, then jams the gun under his own chin.

Murphy closes his eyes as the single, soulless blast of the gun echoes through the basement. Hiro slumps to the floor peacefully, as if he were lying down for much needed rest. Murphy drops the shotgun, wrapping his face in his hands. They'd rather die than have him inside their minds. That's a hard truth that will stick with Murphy for a long, long time.

There's a string of quick buzzes.

It's the phone he got from Ernesto's place. A new series of messages.

Get to the vactrain station. The new, fancy one.

You'll get your destination once you get there.
Tell no one.

"Who the hell are you?" Murphy whispers, cutting through emotions still fresh and raw.

A new realization hits him, knocking him loose from the carnage and the messages from the unknown sender. The cell signal in the house is back up. Murphy races up the stairs, pulling his personal phone.

As he calls in to the CIA emergency line, he moves fast, grabbing towels from the bathroom. He inspects Mother's wounds, describing them to the agent on the line. Every second counts, and if the medic coming can get a head start, then there's a chance. Dressing her wounds the best he can, he knows the CIA will come storming into the safe house in minutes if not seconds.

He looks to the mystery phone with the cryptic messages.

He has to leave. This has to end.

One way or another.

"They're coming, Mother." He brushes her hair away from her eyes. "They'll take good care of you. Hang on, you scary bitch."

Murphy places a pillow from the couch behind her head.

CHAPTER 29

THE NEWARK STATION is bustling at this hour.

Murphy received another message after he parked the car.

There's a ticket waiting for you at the kiosk.

The vactrain ticket says it's taking him to Chicago. Whoever bought the ticket paid for a premium private car and the max acceleration/deceleration upcharge. Murphy's heard these are twice the cost of a normal ticket and the speed makes for a less comfortable ride. Not his favorite, but it means one thing is for certain—the person pulling the strings is on a clock.

This person is concerned that every second matters.

Another message buzzes.

A car is waiting for you on the other end of this joy ride.

The idea of being led around by the nose isn't something Murphy loves either, but he also knows he has to give to get in this situation. Good options are funneling quickly to zero. Murphy takes the ticket and heads toward a small crowd that waits near a platform. His CIA credentials—makes Murphy laugh to think about it in those terms—allowed him to bring his Glock along for the ride as long as it was unloaded. He keeps it tucked behind his back, under his shirt, but the fact it's there gives him some small bit of comfort.

He's fifth in the queue to enter the high-speed train.

He tries to ignore the aches and pains that fire through his body. As the adrenaline fades, the realities of the physical toll of all that's happened is taking hold. On the ride to the station, he received word Mother is in surgery, as well as Darby. The doctors are optimistic, but when you're dealing with bullets along with going under the knife for a considerable length of time, it's hard to predict how the body will react to trauma. Let alone the mind.

Breathing in and out, he clenches his fists and releases them quick in an attempt to unwind his tangled tension. After a few minutes, Murphy's boarding number is called. He heads into the waiting vactrain and is escorted into his private car. The seats are plush with deep leather accented with polished hardwood. They've worked hard to give the illusion of luxury living in a vacuum tube. A modern Orient Express is probably the best way to describe the attempt. There's a harness with thick straps imbedded in the seats that takes away a bit of the luxury veneer, but Murphy knows it is more than necessary.

Murphy straps in, snapping the harness over his shoulders, tucking his feet into the slots under the seat. A notification flashes across the window in front of him coupled with an AI-generated voice that matches the question projected on the glass.

Is Chicago your destination?

"Yes," Murphy grunts, growing tired of talking to these damn machines.

The vactrain has already begun to move forward, swaying slightly side to side.

Distance to destination is 778 miles.

Time to destination is 23 minutes, 37 seconds.

Murphy grips the armrests of the seat. He doesn't enjoy this form of travel. Can't argue with saving time, but it is not his favorite by a long shot. The train begins to move through the underground labyrinth of tunnels on its way to the artery that will send Murphy firing off to Chicago. Strapped into a high-speed form of transport that rockets people around like cattle riding a bullet stuck on a bolt of lightning. A bland, lemon scent fills the car. It borders on antiseptic, but the anti-nausea medication released into the air is also a necessity.

Departing the station in one minute. Heads back, please. Rapid acceleration begins in 59 seconds.

A padded restraint slides out from the top of the seat and extends across Murphy's forehead, holding his neck against the headrest. Murphy thinks of a rollercoaster he loved as a child. Of how the metal bar restraint would come down over him and his skinny frame. He guesses this is something from Noah. A comforting memory that's trying to soothe him.

The train jolts, stops, jolts again and stops, settling into a grove Murphy guesses is the primary tube. He looks through the glass in front of him but there is nothing to see. Complete darkness with a long red light that runs seemingly into an endless horizon.

Three.

Two.

The long light turns yellow.

One.

Green.

Murphy's body feels like it's being sucked deep into the seat. The world is nothing but constant, rushing darkness through the glass. There's no sense of the incredible speed, more like he's being held down by an incredible force. He tries to lift his arms even though he knows it's no use. After a few moments, the acceleration ends and there's no real sense of movement. Only the occasional break in the racing dark that surrounds the glass.

Murphy tries to parse what's happened over the last few days.

An impossible task, he knows.

He needs to focus on whoever is at the end of this ride.

Counting backward, he tries to unspool his tangled thoughts. Attempting to wiggle himself away from his imprisoned mind to find a floating freedom that comes from slipping into the void of a thoughtless state. Needs to empty his bouncing thoughts and find some form of rest. A rested mind will be necessary if he's going to beat whatever is waiting for him.

And whatever is waiting for him will require all that he has.

Suddenly, the car fills with light. A rolling landscape scrolls past as if he's in a movie playing in fast-forward. The world is a mutating blur of shapeless color. Impossible to identify objects or locations. Murphy closes his eyes, continuing his desire to find the thoughtless void.

At least for a little while.

True to the nameless messenger's word, there's a car waiting for him as he exits the station in Chicago.

The sky is dark and cold. A light dusting of snow.

Murphy slides in as the car's warm, comforting voice welcomes him. He's guessing he will not be given the opportunity to switch to a manual driving mode. The car confirms his suspicions are correct when he asks.

Relax and enjoy the trip, Mr. Murphy. We will be in beautiful Buffalo Grove soon.

Murphy knows nothing about Buffalo Grove, but that doesn't mean much. He's hardly an expert in the burbs. Digging deeper, he's pretty sure Mr. Nice Guy doesn't know the area either. He pulls his Glock from behind his back. More to feel it in his hand. He slides in a magazine, a security blanket of sorts.

The car pulls away from the station and onto the highway leaving the city of Chicago. There's comfort in the fact this view is moving at a more normal rate of speed. He can make out the city. The buildings. The faces of people. The neighborhoods. The rich and the poor and the absence of a middle. The heated seats feel good on his battered body. His muscles throb over his aching bones. There's a sandwich on the seat next to him. A nice gesture, but there's no way in hell he's eating or drinking anything provided in this car.

The phone buzzes. Murphy looks to the screen.

The car will take you where you need to be. I'll meet you there.

I'm the woman with a green lizard on her neck.

Green lizard?

On a woman's neck?

Murphy's mind spins, flipping through the database of people who populate his mind. Nothing. No one, male or female, with a lizard. Then, like confirming fingers snapping inside his head, he remembers. The diner. The greatest pie in the world. When he first met Mr. Madness. When he and his friends unleashed their special brand of chaos. There was a woman one table over. She was watching them. A bright-green lizard was tattooed on her neck. He didn't recognize her then and has no idea who she is now.

Murphy leans back into the seat, gripping his Glock, rubbing the barrel with his fingers.

"Son of a bitch."

CHAPTER 30

THE WOMAN with the neon-green lizard neck tat chews the last bite of her burger.

Their cars are parked on the side of an empty dirt road surrounded by trees. She and Murphy stand to the right of a thick patch of woods. Not much can be seen past the first line of trees and brush. The sun has started cutting through offering some heat to balance out the cool breeze that pushes through the branches. Under normal circumstances, a lovely day. There's an earthy scent. The work of fungi and bacteria that decompose plant matter, but there's a different smell in the mix as well. One of caramel and burned sugar.

Murphy has no idea where this appreciation of the outdoors is coming from.

Has to be Mr. Nice Guy.

Murphy begins calculating the likelihood he can pull his Glock and drop her before she gets a shot off. Not out of the question, but he bookmarks the idea, thinking *we're not there yet.*

But we're not far off either.

"Need to walk and talk." She smiles, checks the time, then tosses the empty wrapper inside her car. "That work?"

She raises her empty hands with palms open facing Murphy. A universal showing of *I come in peace.* Murphy knows she has a gun tucked behind her back, much like he does. He can also see the outline of her backup piece on her ankle. This walk and talk will be peaceful, until it's not.

"Not here to fight," she insists.

"No?"

"There's been enough blood spilled. Don't you think?" She puts her hands down, letting them drop to her side like limp noodles. "Not a violent person by nature. I do violence, fully capable and not afraid of it at all, but I don't use it as a traditional go-to. I know it's simply part of the toolbox."

"Got anything in that toolbox to cut the shit?"

"Funny. Heard you were a stitch." Says this with a fading smile. "Listen. We both know we can kill one another. That has been made abundantly clear. But what's in the past can stay there as far as

I'm concerned. I'm here to talk about the future. Wanted you here so we can discuss a future where we are both alive. Thriving. A future together."

"Together? We're only just getting to know one another."

"You're a full snack, Markus Murphy. That's for certain." Smile returns, pouring some syrup on her words.

"You hitting on me, gorgeous?"

"Not today."

"You're kinda horrible at it."

"I'm on a clock."

"Sorry. Hate for you to be late fucking up someone else's life."

"You're about to be on a clock too."

It's the look she's holding so comfortably that eats at Murphy. Like a reckless poker player with shit cards, but a gun under the table. She's holding something, something big.

Murphy's chest tightens.

A constricting feeling that comes from knowing someone you can't trust has agency over you. Not something he embraces. Not that he'd really thought he had much room to manipulate this situation, but he held on to the illusion he at least had a leg to stand on. This woman has all the answers to all the questions he doesn't even know to ask.

"Can we?" She points toward the woods. "Won't take too long. Promise."

"Seems like we're talking fine here." He looks to the sky. "Sun's out. Nice day. Birds and shit."

"There's something you need to see."

"Already got a hole dug in the woods?"

"Just want to talk. Promise." She checks the time again. "And, again, to show you a little something."

Murphy takes a beat. With zero good options, he reluctantly gives her a nod.

They move side by side into the woods, weaving between the trees. She leads mostly but she's conscious to stay near him. Sometimes she drifts back to walking beside him, slightly behind him, then she'll move a few steps ahead.

It's a skill Murphy has learned as well. The ability to watch someone without watching them. The way she moves. The way she speaks. Everything has a purpose. Nothing wasted. Every word and each movement of her body is building toward something for her. This is a person who's been trained. More importantly, she's taken to the training and made it part of who she is.

There's also a pang of familiarity with her as well.

They cut a path through the trees while

moving in silence. He knows she's letting his mind fill the quiet. Allowing him to imagine all the possibilities. It's an effective technique. Leaves crunch under their feet. They move branches aside as needed. Murphy waits for her to say something. This is her show. He doesn't want to push her for information. No reason to seem anxious even if anxiety is clearly warranted here. Information will come.

Let her give.

Give her nothing in return.

"I'm going with Emma, by the way. Emma Cain," she finally says, holding a branch back and allowing him to pass. "My name. Still on the fence about it. What do you think?"

"Nice. Catchy. Going with a kind yet firm sort of thing?"

"Something like that." She skips like a child enjoying the outdoors. "Probably color my hair too. Maybe do something about this lizard tat. It's a bit of an identifier."

Murphy nods. "Makes sense. Planning a trip somewhere?"

"I am. Many somewheres."

They reach a bit of an incline. A small hill. Nothing crazy, but enough to start a burn inside the thighs. Murphy so badly wants to slam her head against a tree and scream questions into her smug face.

Where are we going?

What the hell are you doing?

Who the hell are you?

Emma checks the time again. She turns her focus to an area up ahead. Murphy can see her mind grinding on something. There's a plan. No question. One he's strolling into and there's not much he can do about it. She's working the math. He feels like he's forgotten how to add and subtract.

Murphy grips his fists tight, then releases.

He shakes his right hand, wanting to keep it loose as possible so he can make a quick play for his Glock if he needs to make a move. Wants a lightning-fast, smooth draw if he needs to go full-on Murphy to take on whatever is over this hill.

He can't freeze. Cannot allow a replay of the diner.

"I'm CIA. Former CIA, I guess is more accurate. Even though there was no formal separation," Emma says. "You probably guessed some of that."

Murphy alternates his focus between her hands that sway by her sides and the top of the hill up ahead. Thinks he hears a road nearby. There's a dog barking off in the distance. Maybe the smell of meat on an outdoor grill.

"You escaped the lab with Ernesto. Right? They don't have a record of you."

"True, I did leave the facility with Ernesto, and no, I doubt seriously there's any record of me. Not an accurate one at least." She holds another branch for him. They aren't far from the top of the hill. "I am a lot like you. Did you know that?"

"You used to work with Agent Irving. Didn't you?"

"Very good, Murphy. Heard you were a sharp one."

"You were killed."

"Yeah, died badly, I'm afraid. Hurt quite a bit, but probably deserved some of it."

They're reaching the top of the hill but still unable to see over the edge clearly. She checks the time, then holds up a hand, signaling for him to stop. Murphy slows, digging his feet into the ground. His feet are spread shoulder width, ready to launch or bolt. He previsualizes pulling his gun. Inside his mind, he can hear the gunshots echoing across the woods. One of their bodies falling to the dirt.

"I'm going to say some things to you now." Emma locks in on his eyes. Her mood has shifted from playful to painfully serious. "And what you say in return is so very, very important."

Murphy stares back. Clucks his tongue, then confirms with a nod.

"Like I said, I am a lot like you. I don't share your mind like Mr. Madness or Hiro or even dear Tinker. But I am—what do they call it—a split-head."

Murphy's back stiffens. Spine becoming a steel rod.

Her jacket buzzes. Comes from her inside pocket. She bites her lip and nods, as if the buzz is telling her something she's been waiting to hear.

"Come on. Almost there." She motions for him to follow her up to the crest of the hill.

Murphy's heart pounds inside his chest.

"The only place where Ernesto was ahead of Peyton's work was with the long-term transition of the mind. He figured out how to avoid what Tinker, the others, and perhaps you experienced with—"

"The crashing." He doesn't want to acknowledge anything he's struggled with.

"That's right. Ernesto knew that pure Murphy, meaning you as the alpha, was too much. It wouldn't hold over time when mixed with opposite personalities. Mr. Madness and the others, the ones who shared your mind, they were stable people before you showed up. They had their problems, of course they did, everyone does, but they didn't have Markus Murphy-sized issues." Emma pauses. "You see, Peyton didn't try adding the alpha to others. She didn't add you to multiple people. No, she did the opposite. She added a nice, kind, compassionate human to you. Very different. She's a dutiful scientist. Took it slow. She wanted to help people. Do things the right way. Humane, even."

"God forbid."

Emma shrugs.

As they reach the top of the hill, they can see a modest home below with a high redwood fence surrounding the backyard. From this vantage point, they can see down into the yard with a stretch of road about forty to fifty yards away from the house. A Labrador barks near the rear door of the house. There's a trail of smoke drifting out from an outdoor grill. Smells amazing. Looks and feels like a home most everyone would want to live in.

"You ever get angry?" she asks.

"That a serious question?"

"You're right. Strike that." She resets. "Do you ever feel angry about what they did to you?"

"There a point to this little stroll in the woods?"

"Getting there, but I would really like to know

—do you ever feel angry at them? For what they turned you into. Surely both sides of you are, at the very least, moderately pissed off."

Murphy is all too familiar with the anger she's talking about. That will always be there to some extent, but he's laid it to rest the best he can. He won't let her bait him into something here.

"Like you said, *the past is in the past*."

"Fair enough." Emma checks the time again.

She puts her hands up, motioning, asking permission to reach behind her. Murphy wiggles his fingers, moves his hand in a ready position, then nods. Nice and easy she pulls a pair of high-powered M22 binoculars from behind her back. Murphy knows these. Military grade. Used by the Marines.

What is she up to?

Afraid he already knows the answer.

A black Tesla sedan with blackout windows pulls to a stop on the road that lies up and to the right of the house. Pointing toward the car, she nudges him to take a look through the M22s. Murphy fights his shaking hands, placing them to his eyes. The car window lowers.

Brubaker sits in the passenger side. She stares directly at him. Void of expression.

Everything inside of Murphy stops.

Lungs stop drawing air. Thoughts shut down.

"She's the one who was added to me. Brubaker was put into my mind." She smiles. "Only, I'm the newer model. One created with the lessons learned. Adjustments made from mistakes made. I will not crash. I'm the mix of two similar minds with updated, improved science."

The Tesla's window goes up.

Murphy's hand drops to his side, his fingers barely clinging to the binoculars. As if someone wiped his soul clean from his body.

"And to be clear, I'm someone who was not so nice to begin with."

She checks the time once again, then looks to the house. She gives Murphy another nudge. His lifeless body moves forward a few steps. Emma looks down at his feet. There's a rock with a black stripe painted across it. Murphy's feet are just behind the rock.

"Move closer," she whispers in his ear. "But not too close."

Murphy takes a step, moving past the rock with the black stripe.

"Good." Emma stands behind him speaking in a calm, soothing tone. "You can have the US. We only want the rest of the world."

"What the hell are you talking—"

"Brubaker and I have things set up. Things are in motion. We have lots of friends overseas. Jobs. Big jobs, exciting moves we can make."

"You think I'm going to let you two just bounce out of here?"

"No, I don't. That's why we're here, Murphy." Emma raises Murphy's hand, making sure the M22s reach his eyes one more time.

The door of the house below opens.

Murphy holds his breath.

The man and woman from the park step out carrying two baby girls.

His girls.

"You are now standing within fifty yards of your girls. The CIA will be here in minutes," Emma says, glancing toward the striped rock. "I just need you to know that I know where they are. I wish them no harm. Brubaker doesn't even know they are here. Don't worry, I made sure the sight line from the road can't see into the back-yard. Those girls, that's really her only true weakness."

"I'm going to kill you," he says, voice breaking.

"No, no you're not, and here's why. If I even think you're coming after us, I'm going to carve up everyone in that house. Even the goddamn dog." Emma steps back. "This is a peace offering,

Murphy. A chance. An opportunity for you to do the right thing."

"You set up the ambush at the safe house." His eyes close.

She nods. Checks the time one last time. The CIA will be there soon.

"You wanted everyone focused on the attack at the safe house. Made it easier to get Brubaker out of the hospital."

"*Easier*, but not easy."

"You wanted us all to kill one another."

"You're running out of time, Murphy."

"You wanted Mr. Madness, Tinker, Hiro to kill as many of us as possible. Wanted us to kill them. Then, you'd deal with whoever was left."

"Needed a result. An answer so I could form a reasonable, properly measured action. Somehow, I always knew you'd be the last one standing."

Emma shrugs, shoving her hands into her pockets.

What's a girl to do?

"If I'm being honest, it was more like we ran out of time. I wanted to kill you today. Knew you'd be a tough out, love a challenge, really hoped Brubaker and I could do it together. Kill you, start clean, and it would be this little bonding experience for us. But, there's a bit of a soft spot when it comes to you. Guess we both have it in a way. However, that bitch they stuck in her head gnawed away some of her edge."

Murphy moves toward her.

Emma waves a finger at him, then points to the girls laughing, playing in the yard below. The dog runs between them. The man and woman have smiles so big they can be seen even from where they stand.

"Brubaker and me? We're so alike and so different at the same time. Like sisters in that way."

Murphy watches the girls. His girls. Feels something inside unhinge.

"If you touch them—"

"Murphy—"

"—you better kill yourself before I get to you."

"Come on, now."

"Tell me you understand what I'm saying to you, Emma Cain."

"Oh, I understand completely, Markus Murphy. But you need to understand the beauty of what I'm saying to you. None of us—you, me, or your girls—none of us have to die or experience an ounce of pain. You are in absolute control of that." Emma snaps her fingers, bringing his hard stare back to her. "Do not give me a reason to come back here."

Murphy pulls his Glock.

Green means go.

Emma flips three small injectors before he can level his weapon. Two in his neck. One in his chest. Murphy feels himself peel away from the world upon impact. He rips the one from his chest. His knees give out and he slumps down into the crunching leaves as he reaches for his neck.

Emma pulls his arm back, away from the two injectors, while easing him down.

He remembers the night in New York when he did the same thing to Brubaker. Flipped the same injectors into Brubaker's neck, putting her down in the street like a wild animal.

His eyes lower like thick doors made of lead.

Emma leans down, stuffing something into his jacket.

"Easy now," she whispers, her lips close to his ear. "You've done good. Time to rest. Time to carve out some peace for yourself."

Murphy fumbles to hold on to consciousness that's sliding away from him. His fingers dig into the grass as he tries to drag himself closer to her. Globs of light collect, swallowing his vision.

"Wait?" slips from lips.

Emma Cain waves goodbye, then skips away toward the Tesla. And Brubaker.

His mind screams like a madman. Veins pulp and pop along his neck while his body lies motionless, seemingly to sink into the ground underneath him.

His fingers release the grass as the dark takes hold.

3 WEEKS LATER

Murphy chews on a slice of pizza as he towels off from his shower.

His work uniform is spread out flat-guy style across the bed.

A bed he still hasn't gotten proper sheets for yet.

There's a pair of secondhand-store jeans, a navy-blue T-shirt, black workout socks and a pair of high-dollar sneakers that cost more than a car payment. The T-shirt has the words Johnny Psycho's written in some form of bloodred neon font on the front. A cartoonlike logo of two hands firing off double-barrel middle fingers on the back.

Johnny was kind enough to give Murphy his job back. Well, he only worked there for an hour or so, and his hiring was really because the feds leaned on Johnny pretty hard, but it was long enough for Murphy to show what he could do. Aside from almost killing a couple of assholes while working the front door, Murphy demonstrated some skills behind the bar.

Behind a bar is where Murphy has found the most comfort since all this started.

It was only for a moment—only a blink in time, really—but Murphy felt a calming connection with the rhythm of the work. The feel of being the eye of the storm, without the anxiety of constant death. As brief as it was, it was refreshing to see how everyday working people lived. Murphy had never tended bar, or even ever had a real job per se, but Mr. Nice Guy was a pro at slinging sauce.

Looking back, that was the first time the two blended. Their minds mixed together during their time at the bar, and it was at a time when they had no idea that was what was happening to either of them. It was before Peyton explained their new lives. Crazy to think of it as a simpler time, but it was without question before everything turned upside down and was lit on fire.

There was comfort in the ignorance of the madness to come.

Also, working at Johnny Psycho's makes perfect sense considering Murphy has no real marketable skills other than murder and mayhem. All these points made it a pretty easy decision to reach out to Johnny when Murphy hit New York.

Johnny—the gravy-voiced proprietor of Johnny Psycho's—hid any reluctance he might have had and hired Murphy on the spot. They'd hit it off when they met that first night, before things traveled north of crazy. Murphy made it clear he was a bartender and had no interest in muscling drunks or working the door. Johnny agreed but made him promise that if things went shithouse with a full-on bar brawl Murphy would jump in and crack skulls if needed.

Murphy thought that was fair. So far the tips have been good, and the clientele and coworkers have been okay. It hasn't been long, but it feels like he's settling into a version of normal. Something that some people might consider an honest life. A simple life. Simple and honest sounds nice. That was the entire point of his move to the city.

New York City.

A place he could disappear into.

Pulling on his clothes, he tells the wall screen to shut off some random cooking show that's been playing in the background as he got ready for work. He can't watch the news. Music only jars loose memories or makes him want to dance—odd but true—and he's found the lull of people arguing while cooking shit to be perfect white noise for him. He slides his Glock behind his back until he feels the soft click of the holster. Adjusting his T-shirt, he grabs an ID that says he's Blake Harper from Hoboken, along with a couple of the prepaid credit cards the CIA gave him.

He knows it's all closely monitored. The ID, the cards, Blake Harper, Murphy, his mind and body, all of it. Everything he's done or will do has been and will be watched, analyzed to death, and dissected. Not much he can do about it, so Murphy tries to find peace with it. Tells himself it's like he's a global superstar sensation and the CIA is the paparazzi. All bullshit, but it gets him through the day.

None of this is perfect.

Perfect is unobtainable.

The agency was kind enough to set him up with some funding to get him started on this new life of his. Allowed him to get into this New York apartment and pick up a few things. Got himself a good bed, a so-so couch, and the best media setup he could find. Also bought three plates, four cups, and two bowls. A pan. A pot. Four sets of forks and spoons, along with a butcher block of high-end knives. He figured the knives could serve multiple purposes. There's a baseball bat in most rooms, his assault shotgun in the hall closet, a Ka-Bar secured under the bed, and he sleeps with his Glock under his pillow.

His work uniform is oddly similar to his everyday garb.

It's by design. Less decisions. Less to think about. A nice compromise between the minds of Murphy and Mr. Nice Guy. Murphy can appreciate the military aspect of a uniform—although he's come to enjoy nice clothes—and Mr. Nice Guy Noah likes the casual, unpretentious feel of it. The closet holds a variety of black and navy-blue T-shirts, jeans, a good winter coat and a lot of sneakers.

He's found he likes sneakers. Nice ones. Expensive ones. Doesn't mind a cheap T-shirt, but for some reason, he feels the need to pay up for footwear. Maybe it's from his time spent racing through city streets and unknown terrain. From having to go from zero to a hundred at a moment's notice. Rarely go wrong with a nice pair of athletic footwear.

He doesn't really care about the reason why.

Figures he's earned some fucking cool shoes.

He blends into the masses that fill the street as he steps out from his building and into the chilly air. The horde of New Yorkers moves like a rolling river pouring out to destinations that vary from as close as a few blocks away, to the Bronx, to Staten Island, to Philadelphia or everywhere in between. A setting sun lowers like a fireball, hiding between the towering stacks of rock and metal that line the city. A cool, bordering on cold, breeze blows. Murphy jams his hands into his pockets.

He didn't tell them anything about Emma Cain.

Or Lady Brubaker.

During the hours of debriefing, he held to his story that was led to the house near the woods and was attacked from behind by someone unknown. Explained that he had no idea the girls lived there —that much was true—and told them he had no intention of ever going back there.

That was also true, to a certain extent.

The CIA extended their radius, their leash on Murphy. If he gets within one mile of the girls, or the man and woman who adopted them, the CIA will be notified. The alert level will intensify as he moves closer to them. If he gets within a hundred yards, a full-on assault team will be sent in. Murphy seriously doubts they would have the time to scramble a team in time if he were so inclined to try and test it, but he gets what they're saying.

So, that's why Mother lives slightly over a mile away from the girls now.

She finally got out of the hospital—still needs a surgery or two after that attack at the safe house—and she checks in on the girls from time to time. Peyton told Murphy they weren't tracking Mother, at least not yet. *A blind spot in the chaos*, Peyton called it.

Murphy didn't tell Peyton about Emma Cain either.

He did, however, tell Mother. Which is why her relocation was such an easy sell. Murphy told her everything Emma said to him. The threat that was made abundantly clear.

After he finished, Mother paused, took a sip of coffee, then her eyes went cold. "If those bitches fuck with those girls, they better stop worrying about you and start worrying about me."

Murphy had never been more afraid of his mother.

While Peyton didn't press him too much on the how or why of what happened, she did have questions about the severed hand that was found in his jacket. The severed hand of Ernesto. The one that unlocked the box Murphy had in his car. Murphy told her he found the box at Ernesto's place and took it after his run-in with Agent Irving. The hand he was clueless on. There was some borderline truth to those statements as well.

Inside the box was Ernesto's data and findings from all the work he'd done. Most of it was flawed or matched a lot of what Dr. Peyton already knew, but there was some interesting research around the "crashing" issue. Peyton matched his work with what she already had completed, a path she had already stared down with the temporary solution she gave to Murphy at the diner.

The findings were so simple it pissed her off. She was able to create a prescription cocktail that included the advanced Selective Serotonin Reuptake Inhibitor Peyton had been working on, modified to fit Murphy's special circumstance, along with what amounted to a blend of pseudoephedrine and concentrated ibuprofen.

Dr. Peyton couldn't believe she let the simplicity of a solution get bullied by the stubborn belief the answers must be something more complex. It happens with the best of analytical minds. A more intense treatment might become necessary for Murphy down the line, but for now, a daily dose of this combination of medications—along with weekly therapy sessions—and Murphy will be considerably more stable. Still a machine built for murder and mayhem, but one far less glitchy or volatile.

Murphy takes his place behind the bar at Johnny Psycho's.

He breathes in deeply, placing his palms flat on the bar, feeling the nooks and crannies. He loves these private moments before a shift. He presses his fingertips harder and harder, searching for calm in the storm.

"Hey, Harper."

Murphy snaps out of his trance. Almost forgot what they call him here. He smiles as the waitress passes by the bar.

She moved to New York from Colorado to study design a couple of years ago. Right-handed but can use her left remarkably well. Runner. Smart. Capable of shifting between charming and tough seamlessly when it comes to the customers. Murphy has been cold with her—to be fair, he's kept everyone at arm's length since he's gotten here—but she's wearing him down. She's the only one at the bar, other than Johnny, he's said more than six words to.

"Hey, Zoe." Makes it eight words, with a more boyish giggle than he'd like.

"Try not to kill anyone tonight."

Zoe disappears into the back. She was working

the night Murphy beat down a few mountains of muscle while working the front door. He's been trying to downplay the events of that night, but Zoe thinks it is great fun to bust his balls about it.

"She's cute as hell."

Murphy turns, finding Margo Darby sitting at the bar.

"Two bourbons, please." She slides a card toward him. "Keep it open."

Darby looks pretty good considering what happened to her. There are some wounds that are still healing on her face. Souvenirs of her car being attacked near the safe house. As she slides off her jacket, she reveals a few more scrapes and scratches that run along her ridiculously toned triceps. Murphy knows deep down Darby loves showing off her arms even more now that they have battle scars.

He gets it. Those arms and scars say a ton without uttering a word.

"The good stuff?" Murphy asks. "We have some almost drinkable, moderately priced stuff under the bar. I know you're a government worker so—"

"The good stuff is fine. Thank you."

Murphy one-hands two glasses while grabbing a bottle he keeps under the bar for himself.

"What brings you to New York, Special Agent Darby?"

"Been thinking."

"Sounds awful."

"When you left Ernesto's place, how did you know to go to the safe house?"

"No hello?" Murphy pours, then pushes a glass toward Darby. "No *how ya been, man?*"

"We have the records from the car. How fast you went. How you went straight to the location without a hint of hesitation."

"Irving."

"Irving's face was crushed. The closer was still on when we found what was left of his face. He couldn't tell you a damn thing, unless you put that on him."

"I did not."

"Okay, so—"

"He wrote it down. I found an old-ass legal pad and got him to spill what he knew."

"Of course." Margo snaps her fingers. "Do you have that piece of paper? For the file. Would be a big help. Ya know, to close things out."

"I'll look. Might have lost it during all we've been through."

"Right." Sips her drink, letting it coat her

tongue before swallowing it down. "What do you know about Brubaker's escape?"

"I know what you know. A ton of nothing."

She leans in. "What are you hiding, Markus Murphy?"

"I'm an open book, Margo Darby."

Darby nods. They drink. Neither one giving anything.

"You like working here?" She looks around. "This what you want to do with your life?"

"Very much so."

"Might get bored. Exciting guy like you."

"Like to try out bored for a while."

"Okay. Try this on." Darby places her elbows on the bar, folding her hands under her chin. "There's work I can offer you. Projects, if you will. You pick and choose what interests you. Off the books. Autonomous, Murphy-driven gigs. Perhaps, just maybe, start with the person, or persons, you won't talk—"

"Flattering, but no thank you. Like it here."

"Think about it? You can only flirt with waitresses for so long."

"Pretty sure I just told you what I thought."

"Come on, Murphy."

"How about fuck no?"

"You have to be a little curious. Right?"

"If you were right, I'd agree. But since you're not—" Murphy downs his drink.

"One more?" Darby asks.

"Think we've had enough." Murphy pushes her card back. "On the house."

"Okay." Darby grins, taking her card back. "Take care of yourself, Murphy."

Murphy watches Darby disappear, swallowed up by the growing crowd. His shoulders creep up to his ears like earrings. His chest tightens. Fights to find an easy breath. The life he's tried to suppress, the thoughts he doesn't want, come flooding into his battered mind. Blurring fragments of moments. Faces of Brubaker and of Cain. The horrible sound of Irving's bones crushing on the dirty floor at that house. Gunshots ring and rattle inside his head. The two bullets that took the lives of Hiro and Tinker. Two people who didn't want to live with Murphy's thoughts either. Rage pumps like poison through his pounding heart. He pours himself another drink. Slams it down immediately.

"Easy there, killer." Zoe stands across the bar. "It's early."

Her playful name—*killer*—slides into the meat of Murphy's mind like a switchblade.

"Hey." Zoe scrunches her nose. "You okay, man?"

"No." He holds her eyes.

"Okay." She presses her lips together and nods, not needing to dig for answers.

Reaching under the bar, he pulls out a new, clean glass. Pours a healthy pour of the good stuff, slides it toward her, then treats himself to another. Zoe raises her glass. Murphy raises his.

"Let's drink to..." Fake struggling to come up with a toast, she works that wonderful smile. "Good booze and simpler lives."

The tension he drags around drops. Shoulders ease down. Murphy smiles back, genuinely, as if he's given himself permission to exhale. He thinks of what Emma Cain last said to him.

You've done good.

Time to rest. Time to carve out some peace for yourself.

"Absolutely."

Coming in the summer of 2021. Book 3 in the Markus Murphy series.... PERFECT MONSTERS.

ABOUT THE AUTHOR

 Mike has been a bartender, dish-washer, investment analyst, and an unpaid Hollywood intern. He's quit corporate America, come back, been fired, promoted, fired, and currently he writes stories about questionable people making questionable decisions. Keep up with Mike at...

www.mikemccrary.com

mccrarynews@mikemccrary.com

I say the same thing with each book and will continue saying it until it stops being true... you can't do a damn thing alone. So, I'd like to thank the people who gave help and hope during this fun and occasionally nutty writing life.

If you're reading this right now, you deserve the biggest thank you of all. Even if we've never met, you've been cool and kind enough to grab a copy of my book and give it a read. That there, my dear, friendly, gorgeous reader deserves one big as hell ACKNOWLEDGEMENT.

Thanks, good people.

If you keep reading. I'll keep writing.

Mike McCrary